THE CALL OF THE COLLECTIVE

PAUL ORTON

Copyright © 2024 Paul Orton

The right of Paul Orton to be identified as the Author of the Work has been asserted by him in accordance with the Copyright, Designs and Patents Act 1988.
All rights reserved.

Apart from any use permitted under UK copyright law, this publication may only be reproduced, stored or transmitted, in any form, or by any means with prior permission in writing from the copyright holder or in the case of reprographic production in accordance with the terms of licences issued by the Copyright Licensing Agency and may not be otherwise circulated in any form of binding or cover other than that in which it is published and without a similar condition being imposed on the subsequent purchaser.

All characters in this publication are fictitious and any resemblance to real persons, living or dead, is purely co-incidental.

Cover Design by James, GoOnWrite.com

Font used for title page and chapter headings:
'Bellfort Rough Demo' © Bartek Nowak, used under licence.

PROLOGUE

Zac. Jamie. I don't know who I am.

After a few weeks in Arcadia, everything feels different. Unreal.

The people are nice. Most of them, anyway. But I'm meant to be spying on them, finding a hidden device so the Resistance can hack their network. To the people here, I'm Jamie, the twelve-year-old nephew of the founder, Aaron Greaves. They think I came to live here after my mum was taken away.

But, to the Resistance, I'm Zac, the last hope. Everyone is counting on me, waiting for me to complete my mission. Only if I take down the Collective can we hope to release the vaccine to Vicron-X, bringing an end to the lockdown. That's what I came here to do.

But what they want me to do isn't easy.

Nothing ever is.

The longer I spend here, the harder my mission feels.

Sometimes I wonder if I've been set an impossible task.

But I still need to do it.

My name is Zac.

I just have to hope no one finds out.

ONE

I'm running out of time.

My efforts become more frantic as I scrabble in the stream.

There must be a thousand rocks in here and they all look the same. I don't know how I'm ever meant to find the one that the Resistance have catapulted over the fence, the one that has a copy-token inside.

Trees surround the small clearing. The place smells of moss and damp earth. Birds chirp loudly overhead.

But the light is fading fast. I wasn't expecting to be out this long. If I don't head back soon, I'll be stumbling through the forest in the dark.

The cold water rushes around my ankles, my trainers submerged. I've had enough.

I climb out, squelching my way over the rocks.

My smart band beeps insistently and I check the display: *no movement detected.*

I need to go.

Now.

Otherwise, they'll send out a search and rescue party, and that will lead to a lot of questions.

I curse under my breath as I take one last look behind me.

When Layla explained the plan to me, back at Resistance headquarters, it sounded brilliant. No one could sneak technology into Arcadia, but anyone could lob a rock over the fence. All I had to do was pick it up on the other side.

Now, though, the plan seems stupid.

How am I ever going to locate the particular rock that contains the copy-token? All the stones look the same. They're grey and smooth, just like the one I'm looking for.

Without that rock, I'll never be able to hack into the Collective network and provide the Resistance with the access they need to end the lockdown.

I have to find it.

But not today.

Right now, I need to get back to the settlement before anyone wonders where I am.

I make my way to the path, then set off at a steady pace. As soon as I start moving, I warm up.

The clothes help. Other than the plain black trainers, I'm only wearing two things: a top that clings to my body and a pair of tights that cover my entire bottom half, even my feet. They're black with a red stripe down either side. I may look weird, but I'm not complaining; the active wear is comfortable, and it does a great job of regulating body temperature. Besides, everyone wears this stuff in Arcadia.

I check my smart band. The warning message has disappeared, replaced by a readout of my distance, time, and the number of calories I've burned.

That's a relief. The system knows I'm on the move. No one will think I've twisted my ankle or broken my leg and come looking for me. But I wish I could take a walk through the woods without being tracked.

Exercise is a big thing here. The smart bands are part of the standard uniform. They upload your stats to a central computer. Then, you get advice as to what exercise you have to do to stay fit. Well, if you're under eighteen, it's not really advice; it's an expectation.

I've had to run over 5k every day since I've been here. I don't mind all that much; I used to run further in the Resistance. Still, it's another thing to fit into the hectic schedule.

It takes me twenty minutes to reach the red boundary. Once I pass the markers, I run past tree houses and log cabins. Wooden walkways hang in the air, connecting them to one another, making the development a part of the forest, part of nature.

The path takes me to the edge of the lake, the dark blue water mirroring the sky.

Nearly there.

My tired muscles complain as I jog up a ramp and climb some steps to get to the upper level. Once I'm there, I cross a narrow bridge, clinging to the handrail. When I first arrived, I found it scary being up this high, but I soon got used to it. When you live in a place like this, you have to.

Besides, the views are spectacular. I can see right over the lake from here. Even though it's dusk, some kids are out on kayaks, splashing each other with their paddles. Further still, I can see a few cabins on the opposite shore; the edge of another zone.

I live in a tree house with a man called Aaron Greaves, who thinks he's my uncle. Our place is bigger than most. It looks like someone built it onto the trunk. This isn't some kid's den. It's all glass walls and balconies, something that wouldn't look out of place in the architects' magazines my mum used to leave lying around.

The thought of Mum makes me pause. She was arrested for helping the Resistance find out about this place, and now she's in prison somewhere, out in the real world, along with my brother. I have to finish what she started. That's why I'm here.

I push open the door, stepping into the clean, modern hallway. There's not a lot of furniture; just a rack for shoes. Kicking off my trainers, I pad through to my bedroom in my damp tights, leaving wet footsteps on the polished floor.

"Is that you, Master Jamie?" calls out a voice. It's Maddie, the housekeeper.

"Yeah. Sorry I'm late. I got a bit lost. I'm gonna

take a shower." I slip inside my room and close the door before she can reply.

Maddie's alright. She's a friendly sort, always taking care of me and cooking and cleaning for me and my uncle. But she also asks a lot of questions. I don't know if she's nosy or if she's been told to keep an eye on me. Either way, I'd rather not be interrogated right now.

I look around. My room is always clean. It's shaped like an upside-down V, the sloping walls making the floor much bigger than the headspace. On one side is a single bed. On the other is a narrow desk with a smart computer and some cleverly concealed cupboards.

The far wall is actually a giant window that looks out towards the lake. At this end, there's my own private bathroom.

I strip off the dirty clothes. I can see a red bump on my arm where I was injected with the vaccine for Vicron-X. The Resistance were right about that: the Collective do have it and they are keeping it from the outside world, but I still haven't worked out why.

I step into the shower, desperate to wash off the dirt and sweat from another long day.

I'm barely under the water before there's a knock at the door.

What now?

"Master Jamie?"

"What? I told you I'm taking a shower."

"It's your uncle. He wants to see you as soon as you're done. Make it quick."

"Sure, ok."

Uncle Aaron is not someone you leave waiting.

And I can't help wondering why he wants to see me.

Does he know where I've been and what I'm looking for?

Worse still, does he know who I really am?

TWO

It's properly dark by the time I wander on to the balcony. Pretty lights are strung up around the supports, making it feel a bit like Christmas, even though it's late spring.

Aaron is sitting at the table, his piercing blue eyes focused on his tablet. He's probably much older than he looks: his well-trimmed beard has flecks of grey, but he has a full head of hair and the body of a twenty-year-old.

I hesitate by the glass door. "You asked to see me, Uncle?"

"Two minutes."

I wait for him to finish.

Finally, he puts down his tablet and gestures to a chair. "Sit, Jamie."

I obediently slump into the seat opposite. I

figure if my mission is going to succeed, I have to stay on the right side of Aaron Greaves. As one of the founders of the Collective, and the man who first envisaged Arcadia, he's a powerful guy.

"Am I in trouble?" I blurt out.

He gazes at me, not giving anything away. "Have you done something wrong?"

"I don't think so."

Aaron picks up his drink and takes a sip, never taking his eyes off me. "You're late home."

"Yeah, sorry about that." I shift uncomfortably in my seat. "I went for an extra run and got lost. It took me a while to find my way back."

"An extra run?" There's a note of surprise in his voice. "Is your exercise schedule too relaxed?"

If I don't tread carefully, he's going to increase my workload. I have to get this right.

"No. It's really tough. I barely made my time this morning. But just this once, I wanted a more relaxed run, you know? To enjoy nature without being in such a hurry. That's ok, isn't it?"

"You missed supper."

"I'll apologise to Maddie," I assure him.

"You'll do more than that. From tomorrow, you'll help out a bit more around here. You can empty the waste."

Great. Another chore. That's all I need.

I bite my lip, careful not to say anything I'll regret.

"You've gone quiet," he points out.

"It's just so hard, fitting everything in."

"You had time for a relaxed run in the woods. You can't be that hard-pressed."

I sigh and look out over the lake. "I guess. But between lessons, homework, activities and community service, I barely have time to breathe."

That much is true. The thing that has most surprised me here is the level of intensity. When I first arrived, the place looked like paradise. I imagined we'd spend most of our time relaxing in the sun, not rushing from one thing to another.

"If we want to make Arcadia work, we have to make sacrifices." He sounds distant as he says it, as if this is about more than me. "Everyone here works hard. You need to step up."

"I'm doing my best."

He leans towards me, his cool blue eyes staring into mine. "Listen, Jamie, I know it's not easy. It must be something of a shock moving here, but I can't go easy on you just because you're my nephew. People are already mad I brought you here."

That's news to me.

"Why?" I ask.

"This isn't the kind of place you just invite your family to," he explains. "I broke some rules, getting you here. Don't let me down."

"I'll try not to." I stand up, assuming the conversation is over.

Aaron narrows his eyes. "I haven't dismissed you yet."

"Sorry." I drop back down, confused. It's taken some time to get used to the rules. He's much stricter than my mum.

"There's one more thing. I spoke with the professor earlier. He hasn't been all that impressed with your homework."

Now, I can't hide my frustration. "He expects the impossible!"

"Nevertheless, you will rewrite your last essay to an acceptable standard and you will submit it in the morning."

"Tomorrow? But it'll take hours."

"Then you best get started."

"That's not fair."

His eyebrows furrow. He's not used to people answering back. "Fair or not, it's what you will do. And if I discover that you've handed in anything second-rate, then you will regret it."

"Ok. I'll get on it. Can I go now?"

I'm keen to get out of there before he adds anything else to my to-do list.

"Jamie, I know you must hate me right now, but I'm just trying to help you reach your potential. The world is changing, and this is not the moment for us to slack off. You're a bright boy, but you've grown lazy during lockdown. It's time to change gear."

I don't reply, too scared to tell him what I really think. This man is obsessed and I have no desire to be his latest project.

There's an awkward silence.

Aaron can see we've reached an impasse, and he waves his hand. "You can go."

I get up from the table and make my way back inside, careful not to slam the door.

Maddie is drying up dishes at the sink, humming a tune. Long ginger curls cascade to her shoulders. She's older than my mum, but not by much. She's the only person I've seen in Arcadia who appears overweight.

"Sorry I missed supper. I didn't mean to be so late."

"It's ok, Master Jamie. I saved you some." She presses buttons on the microwave.

"That's really kind. You didn't have to."

She glances at me, a twinkle in her eye. "Next time I won't. That'll be a lesson for you to be more punctual."

I give a weak smile. "Come on, Maddie, you wouldn't let a boy starve."

She just rolls her eyes and we wait a minute longer for the meal to warm through. She pulls it out and puts it on the table. It's some kind of veggie-burger and I tuck in, feeling the need to replace the calories I've burned.

"What did your uncle say?" she asks.

"He wants me to help out more. To take out the waste."

"In that case, you better take it first thing in the morning."

"And I have to rewrite an essay this evening."

"But it's nearly bedtime."

"Try telling him that."

She shakes her head and doesn't respond. She knows as well as I do that trying to get my uncle to change his mind is a waste of time.

And we're both short enough of that as it is.

THREE

I yawn as I pad into the kitchen.

Maddie states the obvious. "You look tired."

"That's probably because I was up until midnight rewriting a stupid essay." I wonder if I've said it too loud. I glance at the sliding door that leads out to the balcony.

Maddie winks at me. "It's ok. He's gone to work."

I relax and settle in a chair, my head in my hands. "I just want to sleep."

"I know." She pours some juice into whatever concoction she's been making in the blender, then presses a button. When it stops, she pours the contents into a glass, which she hands to me. "This might help."

"Thanks." I sip the pink liquid. It's thick and

sweet. I look up in surprise. "This is good."

"It's your uncle's favourite. It does wonders for restoring blood sugar when you're tired."

I happily drink the rest, gasping with satisfaction as I put the glass down.

"Feel better?"

"A bit," I admit. "So, what's for breakfast?"

"Muesli, as usual. Or I could do you some toast?"

What I really want is a full cooked breakfast, but in Arcadia, meat isn't on the menu. "Toast would be great."

"Don't you need to take the waste out first?"

I groan. "I'd forgotten about that."

She lifts a big metal container out from under the sink. I walk over and peek inside to see rotting vegetable peelings and leftover food.

"Gross. Where do I take it? Is there a bin somewhere?"

She laughs. "There are no bins in Arcadia, just compost. You need to head down the path towards the tennis courts. A little further on, you'll come to a big metal building. That's the composting shed."

"But that's miles away."

"That's because no one wants to live next to it. Empty that into the big pit inside. And, whatever you do, don't fall in."

"I won't." I grab the container and head for the door. "One more question. Do people in Arcadia ever just sit down and chill?"

She laughs, bustling over to the sink. "I wouldn't know. I certainly don't!"

***

It's difficult to run with the container, so I settle for a brisk walk. It seems to get heavier the further I go, so I keep swapping it from one hand to the other.

The tennis courts are on the outskirts of the red zone. It's only a five-minute walk, but that seems a long way when you're short on time. When I reach them, I can't see any sign of the metal shed. I press on along the path through the woods. I've never been in this part of the forest. The path snakes between fallen trees and wildflowers and the air smells of damp moss. I wonder if I've taken a wrong turn.

How much further?

Just when I'm about to turn back, I see a green corrugated metal building up ahead. They might call it the composting shed, but it looks more like a barn. It's massive. It's also the ugliest building I've seen since I arrived. I'm glad I'm here in the morning; this place would be creepy after dark.

I push on the metal door and it creaks open. I'm about to step inside, but the overpowering smell of rotting food makes it hard to breathe, forcing me back.

Come on, Zac, get it done.

I take a deep breath and try again. As I enter, a light turns on. That's helpful, because there are no windows. I'm standing on a small wooden platform with a low fence around it. In front of me is a deep pit full of foul-smelling gunk—the compost pit. Insects crawl and worms writhe around in the rotting vegetable peelings. Flies buzz around my head and I swipe at them with my free arm. The sight of so many creepy-crawlies makes me shudder.

I quickly take the lid off the container and tip the contents over the edge, watching them sink into the brown sludge below. Then I dash for the door, gasping for air as I stumble into the warm sunshine.

Well, that's a fun job.

At least the container is a lot lighter now. It shouldn't take as long to get back.

***

Something makes me stop.

I hear movement, hushed voices.

I creep forward, staying hidden behind the trees.

There are two boys, around my age, next to the tennis courts. I know them both; we have lessons together. One of them is a shy lad called Hugh. The other is Tyler, who acts like he owns the place.

Tyler is holding Hugh against the fence, and Hugh's eyes are wide with fear.

I can only hear snatches of the conversation, but Tyler's voice is whispering in a harsh tone. "another mark... fail the assignment... the last thing..."

I can't work out what he's talking about, but I've already seen enough. I step out of the bushes.

"Leave him alone."

Tyler lets go and turns around. He has a face that matches his personality: pinched and cruel. His black hair is brushed backwards, which is meant to look stylish, but just accentuates his spotty forehead.

He smirks when he sees me. "This is none of your business, Jamie," he warns. "Me and Hugh are just having a friendly discussion. Isn't that right, Hugh?"

Hugh nods reluctantly.

"It doesn't look that friendly to me."

"Yeah, well you're the new boy. You don't know how things work here."

"I know you're a bully."

Tyler steps towards me. He's a head taller, and he's solid. If we fight, there's every chance he'll win. "I'm a leader. Hugh is in my gang. Perhaps you'd like to join? I hear you're pretty fast. I could use someone to do my run each day."

"Thanks, but I'll pass."

He smirks as if I've said something funny. "Perhaps you need some time to think about it. In the meantime, if you tell anyone about this, then you'll regret it."

Careful, Zac.

"I'm not scared of you," I say. But my heart is pounding.

"We'll see."

He makes a sudden movement and I flinch, expecting him to hit me. Instead, he ruffles my hair, then walks off.

I rush over to Hugh. "Are you ok?"

He's shaking as he leans against the fence of the tennis court. "You shouldn't have done that."

"Well, you shouldn't let him pick on you."

"You don't know what he's capable of."

"What did he want, anyway?" I ask. "I heard him say something about his assignment."

Hugh doesn't say anything, just rubs his face and looks away.

Then it clicks.

"You do his work?" I can't even imagine how long that would take. I struggle to get my own done in time. "That must take hours."

Hugh nods dejectedly. "You can't tell anyone. Promise?"

I'm torn.

I know that bullies like Tyler only get away with stuff when people are silent, but I don't want to make things worse for Hugh. I also don't want any enemies here. I have enough on my plate, and I need to focus on my mission.

"I won't tell," I say. "At least, not yet."

He seems relieved. "Thanks, Jamie. I appreciate it."

"Come on. Let's get you back."

FOUR

"Your assignment was much better this time," says the professor. I detect a hint of surprise.

Yeah, I'm not as stupid as you think I am.

"Thank you, sir."

"I hope this is a sign of better things to come?"

"Yes, sir."

"You may be seated."

Our classroom is shaped like an octagon. The perimeter wall is made entirely of windows, making the room feel like part of the woods. The only items of furniture are twelve curved white desks, and an additional one for the professor. They're arranged in a circle, facing inwards. Each of them has a screen and computer keyboard built in. The seats are attached to the desks. They're hard and uncomfortable, and don't have a back. There's no way to slouch or scrape your chair here; students are expected to behave.

There are a couple of other classrooms nearby, but they're for younger kids. All the students in my class are aged from twelve to fifteen. When I first came to lessons just over a week ago, I asked one of my new friends, Ahmid, whether these were all the teenagers in Arcadia, but he told me that this was just the class for those in the red zone.

Ahmid sits on my right and on my left is a girl called Freya. Hugh is further round, still looking miserable. Across the room, Tyler scowls at me. I do my best to ignore him.

The professor stands up. He's a tall, older man with a well-trimmed grey beard and a receding hairline. He looks way too old for the futuristic Arcadia clothing. This man should be in flowing robes, like a schoolmaster from Victorian times.

He's certainly as strict. Any messing around here gets you extra work or community service. Last week, one lad got on the wrong side of him and had to spend Saturday sanding down a wooden walkway. It was a horrible back-breaking job, and I'd felt sorry for him as I saw him slaving away. It helped me understand why everyone is usually so well-behaved.

"Good morning," says the professor. "I trust you are ready for another day's learning. We will start by reviewing the essays you submitted over the network on Monday. Most of you made a reasonable attempt at solving a tricky problem." He walks around the perimeter of the circle as he talks. "When the lockdown ends, people will once again start driving cars, placing strain on our delicate eco-system. If we are going to prevent climate catastrophe, we need to stop people from returning to their old habits. This morning, we're going to consider potential solutions. Gavin, you handled the problem from an economic perspective?"

Gavin is one of the older kids, with ginger hair and glasses. He's a nice enough guy, but also a know-it-all. "I thought that the best answer might be to substantially increase the cost of petrol. That would mean people would be keen not to have to travel so far to work. It could be done in a number of stages to give people time to think about moving house."

"What does everyone else think of that?"

asked the tutor, looking around.

"It's a good idea, but what would it do to delivery companies or people whose jobs involved the need to travel?" asks Ahmid.

"I guess they could get a special discount card or something?" suggests Gavin. "It's not perfect, I admit."

"You had a different approach, didn't you, Ahmid?" asks the tutor.

"Well, sir, I think the answer is about investment in the infrastructure for electric cars, and massively subsidising them. The electricity they use could be provided for free or stupidly cheap for the first five or ten years. That would really give people a motive to replace their existing cars. Perhaps that could work in tandem with Gavin's idea, increasing the cost of petrol?"

The professor nods. "We may need a range of approaches for us to be able to solve such a complex problem."

Someone clears their throat on the other side of the room. It's Tyler. He crosses his arms. "It's not that complex, sir."

"Care to enlighten us, Tyler?"

"We should just cut off the petrol supply and

let people deal with it. They'll soon learn to live without their vehicles if they don't have a choice."

The professor stares out of the window, looking thoughtful. "A good point. We may need to take radical action."

I can't believe what I'm hearing. I speak up. "You can't ban petrol. If you did that, thousands of people would lose their jobs overnight. No one would be able to see their relatives. Some kids couldn't get to school. It's stupid!"

The professor turns on me sharply. "I appreciate your contribution, Jamie, but please watch your tone. This classroom is a place where we explore difficult ethical dilemmas. While your passion is commendable, you need to engage in this debate with more reason and less emotion."

"I just don't think you can mess with people's lives like that. It's not fair."

"Fair is a relative concept when a planet hangs in the balance, wouldn't you agree?"

I stay silent.

The professor turns to the girl on my right. "Freya, rescue us from this disagreement. I believe you had a multi-faceted approach?"

"I think we've overlooked the benefits of

cycling," she says. "If everyone used bikes, then emissions cease to be a problem. Only really heavy loads would need to be transported using vehicles."

The lesson continues like that for some time, students voicing their ideas and debating the possibilities. After a while, I tune out. I have more pressing problems to think about, like how I'm ever going to find the fake stone with the copy-token inside.

I wonder whether I can journey out to the perimeter again this evening and take another look. But if I do that, I'll have the same problem as last time.

Also, if I keep hanging around the same location, the data from my smart band might make people suspicious.

They'll wonder why I keep stopping for a long break in the same place every time I go for a run. And my 'uncle' will want to know why I keep disappearing.

But if that's not the way forward, what is?

I need a solution, and fast.

FIVE

"Thought any more about my offer?" mutters Tyler.

We're walking to the sports centre, only a short distance from our classroom.

"What offer?" I ask, confused.

"Whether you want to do my run for me this evening."

"No chance," I mutter. "They'd know, anyway. They trace our smart bands."

He snorts. "That's why we'd swap them."

That's interesting; I hadn't thought about that. If it's possible to give someone else my band, I might be able to sneak off when I need to. But I certainly don't have time to fit in Tyler's exercise as well.

"I'm not doing your run. I already have 5k to

do this evening."

"Let me know if you change your mind. I get the feeling you might." He smirks and barges into me as we make our way through the door.

Great. I've made an enemy. That's all I need.

The sports centre is compact but well-kept. Inside the box-shaped building there's a small gym with various fitness and weight-lifting equipment, a few toilet cubicles and a main sports hall, which works well for team games. That's the part we're using today. There's nothing much in here, just a basketball hoop at either end and some tall windows which have mesh covers to protect them from stray balls.

We come here a lot. Every other lesson is spent in the sports hall or outdoors. When I asked Ahmid about it, he said that was because the Collective put such importance on everyone's health, and also because physical activity makes us more awake and able to learn.

"It's about the way the brain works," he explained. "Normal schools don't actually make good use of the time you're there. They're so keen to cram in lesson time that other stuff gets squeezed out. PE in my old school was only once a week before lockdown. Even though I'm not exactly into sports, I can see that after you've been swimming or playing tennis or whatever, you sit back down to work and you can accomplish so much more because you're fresh. After about two hours of study anyone's brain goes dead so there's no point trying to do more right then. You need a break."

That means we alternate between lessons and physical activities. Because the active wear is suitable for almost anything, we don't usually need to change, which saves a lot of time.

Our coach is waiting, holding a large bag of balls. She looks the part: young, athletic, fit. And, like the professor, she has no trouble keeping the class under control. From the way she speaks, I get the impression she used to be in the armed forces.

"Against the wall," she shouts, and we line up. "This morning we're going to be playing different versions of dodgeball. For our warm up game, you can move anywhere in this hall. If the ball hits you on any part of your body, then you're out and you go and stand against the far wall. You wait there until the game is over. One of you will be throwing the balls. They can't move when they are holding a ball, and they can only throw the balls, not kick them. Any questions?"

"What if it hits the wall or floor before it hits you?" asks Kyle.

"For this warm up game, if the ball hits you, you're out, even if it hit something or someone else first. You need quick reactions. Understand?"

We all nod.

"Do I have a volunteer?"

"Yeah, alright coach. I'll do it." Tyler steps forward.

"I'm going to give you two minutes to get everyone out."

"Easy," grins Tyler. He looks at the rest of us like we're fresh meat.

"I'm glad you think that," says the coach. "Because if you fail you'll be doing fifty press-ups and fifty sit-ups. And anyone he gets out will also be doing those. Understood?"

We nod again, a little less enthusiastic.

The coach empties the balls out. They bounce and roll in every direction. "Everyone ready? Start running. I'll count down from three. If any ball touches you after I blow the whistle, you're out."

We scatter across the hall. Tyler remains where he is, waiting for the signal. I can see him tracking me with his eyes. I couldn't care less. So what if he goes for me first? It's only a game and a few push ups.

The coach blows the whistle and Tyler shoots into action. He's fast on his feet, running from one part of the hall to another, picking up balls and hurling them at anyone who's nearby. Within the first ten seconds, he's already got three people out.

His initial victims dealt with, he now locks me in his sights, sprinting across the hall to where I stand paralysed with indecision. He skids to a stop and scoops up a ball. I try to dart past, but he flings the ball at the back of my legs. It catches me on my calf and I'm surprised how much it hurts.

"You're out," he says, smugly.

"I don't care," I mutter.

I limp over to the far wall. If he thinks I care about a game of dodgeball, he's way off. I stand watching while Tyler bags a few more victories. I have to give it to him: he's pretty skilled.

He jogs to the wall furthest from us and then makes his way back, herding those who remain in the game towards the rest of us who are out. Only a few manage to slip past. He gathers up a couple of balls, ready for action, only a few steps away from where I'm standing.

Everything happens fast. Tyler spins round and throws one ball across the room. Once the coach is looking the other way, he swivels back and fires the other ball at my face with incredible force. It slams my head against the wall, and I fall to the ground in pain.

"Oops, sorry."

The coach blows the whistle as soon as she sees me curled up on the ground with blood pouring out my nose. She rushes over.

"What happened?"

"Stray ball, Coach," replies Tyler. "I was aiming for someone and they dodged out the way and it hit Jamie instead."

I glare at him. "He did it on purpose."

The coach takes my head in her hands so she can take a closer look. "It's just a nosebleed," she says, relieved. "Go and clean yourself up in the toilets. Keep your head tilted back until it stops."

"Yes, Coach." I try to prevent the dripping blood from going all over the hall floor as I walk towards the exit.

Tyler stands behind the coach, smirking. He's gotten away with it, just like he knew he would.

Screw you, Tyler.

I suppress the rage that's building. I can't get distracted by him; I don't have time for schoolboy games.

Out in the real world, everyone is still in lockdown, afraid of the virus. My mum and my brother are locked up somewhere, with no hope of release.

Their only hope is me.

I need to figure out a way to get hold of the copy-token and somehow plug it into the Collective network.

And if I'm honest, I'm not any closer to achieving that than when I first arrived.

SIX

I'm sitting with Freya and Ahmid on the lakeshore, under the shade of an enormous tree, looking out at the sparkling blue water. In the distance, we can see younger kids swimming and splashing about, taking advantage of the lunch break to cool off and have some fun.

After a few hours of lessons, we aren't feeling that energetic. Instead, we munch on our nutrition bars and fruit.

I would have taken another trip to the stream if there was time, but there's no way I'd get there and back in the short lunch break, let alone have time to hunt for the copy-token.

"What are your plans for the weekend?" asks Freya.

"I haven't thought that far ahead," admits

Ahmid. "How about you?"

"Same." Freya lies on her back and looks up at the leaves above. "Things have been so busy lately I don't even have time to *plan* my spare time. How sad is that?"

"Why don't we just chill?"

They look at me as if I suggested we rob a bank.

"You still don't get it, do you?" asked Freya, shaking her head. "Tomorrow, the professor is going to ask us what we have planned for the weekend. If you don't have enough activities booked in, then he schedules you for additional community service."

I look at her, aghast. "You don't even get to choose how you spend your free time?"

"Well, you do. Sort of."

Ahmid comes to my rescue. "You're allowed to do anything you want, as long as it's healthy and productive. But they don't like us to sit around and do nothing."

Now I come to think of it, last week, I had thought it was weird when the professor showed such a keen interest in everyone's plans for the weekend. Now, I understand why. Ahmid and

Freya had invited me to go sailing on the Saturday, and Sunday had been spent cycling and working on one of Ahmid's robots.

"I guess we could go sailing again," says Freya.

Ahmid pulls a face. "I dunno. You know what the professor's like. He doesn't like you doing the same thing every week."

My brain is working overtime. I wonder if there might be a way I can use the time to hunt for the copy-token. "Perhaps we could spend some time in the woods," I suggest, casually.

Freya looks interested. "Doing what?"

"Everything is so crazily busy in Arcadia, I thought maybe we could go for a hike, take a picnic. Or even camp out, away from it all. Then we could have some proper time to chill without people getting on our case."

Freya sits up and looks at me, her eyes shining. "Camping out? That's a great idea! That would be amazing!"

Ahmid nods. "I expect they'd let us do that. It is a proper activity after all. Loads of healthy engagement with nature. A fair amount of exercise walking through the woods. Proper community bonding through being together.

And it sounds fun."

Now that they've agreed with it, I realise the flaw in my plan. "Do any of you have any camping gear?"

"We'll have to see what's in the communal supplies," replies Freya, "but it's the kind of thing they're likely to have. We're big on outdoor pursuits here."

"I noticed," I say, drily.

"Let's take a look now, as soon as we've finished our lunch," suggests Ahmid. "The supplies aren't far from here."

Freya smiles at me. "Camping! Jamie, you're a genius!"

I blush, feeling a little guilty about the fact that I have an ulterior motive. Now I have to make sure we end up in the right location. "I think I know the ideal spot. I went for a long run last week and found this place that was just far enough away from everything else but still near fresh water."

Freya runs her hand through her frizzy brown hair. "I don't mind where we go. I'm just looking forward to a weekend of sunbathing and relaxing for a change."

"I don't think I can even remember how to relax," moans Ahmid.

"I'll teach you," I say. "You start by lying down..."

I gave him a playful push, making him roll on to his side. He smiles and raises his half-eaten apple in the air.

"As soon as I've finished eating this, you're gonna pay for that!"

"Boys!" said Freya, rolling her eyes. "What is it about men that they have to get in fights all the time! It's so primitive!"

Ahmid laughs. "Could you try to sound a bit more superior? I don't think you quite pulled it off."

"Oh yeah?" Freya moves faster than either of us expect. Within seconds, she's sat on top of him, holding his arms. Ahmid writhes around, laughing.

"Any other comments you'd like to make?" she asks, raising her eyebrows.

"Just one," he says, a mischievous grin on his face. "Who's primitive now?"

She takes what's left of the apple out of his hand and forces it in his open mouth so he can't speak. "That's better."

"You two, get a room!" I say, shaking my head.

"Ah, Jamie's feeling left out," teases Ahmid. "Don't worry, we love you too!"

"Thanks."

Freya stands up and brushes herself off. "Much as I'd love to stay here all day, teaching you some manners, we ought to go and check the supplies cabin."

Ahmid gets to his feet. "Agreed. Let's go."

***

The cabin is located in the centre of the red zone, not far from our classroom. Inside, there are several rows of shelves, stacked from floor to ceiling with everything you can imagine: sports equipment, mobility aids, musical instruments, specialist cooking devices. It's hard to see what some things are as they're in boxes or other packaging.

Just like in the compost shed, there are no windows. The space is lit by LED strips, but it still feels gloomy, like an abandoned warehouse.

"Why's it so dark in here?"

"Daylight can damage equipment," explains Ahmid.

"Who owns all this stuff, anyway?"

"We all do," says Freya. "That's why it's a *communal* store. You take what you need, when you need it. It means we don't have to keep everything in our cabins all the time."

"Makes sense," I admit grudgingly. It certainly helps to explain why the tree house has so little clutter.

Freya locates a clipboard hanging on the wall. She lifts it off and rifles through a few pages. "Here we are. Tents. N5 apparently."

The racks have letters and the shelves have numbers, so finding the right location is relatively easy. Sure enough, a short way along the shelf is an assortment of tents—all different shapes and sizes.

"This one says that it sleeps 3-4 people," said Ahmid, lifting out a blue bag, "and it's not too heavy."

"Perfect," said Freya. "Let's take that! This camping trip is on! What else do we need?"

I rack my brain. I used to go camping, before the lockdown, but that was years ago.

"Sleeping bags?" I suggest. "Roll mats? And hiking rucksacks?"

Freya scans the list, shouting out letters and numbers to help me and Ahmid find the items. We soon have a large pile.

"What do we do now?" I ask, checking my smart band for the time. "We don't have time to take this stuff back to our cabins. Our next lesson starts in seven minutes."

"That's ok," says Freya. "We'll just pile it in this corner. No one will mind if it's there for a few days." She writes out a polite note explaining that it's being used at the weekend and puts our names at the bottom. "Right, we'd better get back."

I feel a sense of hope and excitement as we hurry across the glade towards our classroom. Not only does a weekend camping with Freya and Ahmid sound fun, but it should also give me the opportunity I need to look for the fake stone.

For the first time since I arrived, I have a plan.

Things are back on track.

SEVEN

"Where did you learn to code like that?" The professor leans over my shoulder to examine the screen more closely. "This is impressive."

Careful, Zac. Don't give anything away.

I can hardly tell him I took computing lessons with the Resistance.

"I mostly taught myself. And one of the teachers at my old school was really into it, so he set up a computer club." I feel myself going red, the lies making me blush. I hope he doesn't notice.

"You say you're developing some sort of virus?"

"That's the plan."

When I was given the option to choose what I wanted to work on for my computing project, that's what I went for. I wasn't sure the professor would approve, but he seemed happy with the idea. I'm hoping that by working on it, I can ask innocent questions about the Arcadia network without raising too many suspicions.

"What does this subroutine do?" The professor lifts a bony finger to point at the screen.

"It copies the virus code to another directory, so there's a backup if the initial application is deleted."

"That's very clever."

"Thank you, sir."

Since I arrived in Arcadia a few weeks ago, I've been surprised how much time we spend programming. At least two hours a day are spent creating algorithms and subroutines, working on complicated projects. Not everyone is working on a virus, though. Freya's working on some kind of artificial intelligence, while Ahmid's program has something to do with robotics.

I'm not complaining about the amount of time we spend on it. Coding is something I've always enjoyed, ever since the Resistance started to teach me. Here, though, it feels different: the cool, airy classroom provides a calm place to focus compared to the cramped and busy pub.

"Can I ask a question, sir?"

"That's what I'm here for, Jamie."

"I'm worried that when I test my virus, it will take down the network in Arcadia. It's pretty potent code."

Just across from me, I can see Tyler looking at his friend Kyle, raising his eyebrows: *just who does this kid think he is?*

Fortunately, the professor doesn't think it's a stupid question.

"You needn't worry about that," he explains. "To start with, each zone in Arcadia has its own network. They're isolated from one another, so if one goes down, the others aren't affected. And it's almost impossible to take one down, anyway."

"But surely they all connect to the internet? They must be connected in some way?"

He gives a small shake of his head. "Actually, no. The red zone's network isn't connected at all. That's why you can't use the computer in your dwelling to search for websites, or buy things, or message people outside Arcadia. You can't even contact someone in the blue zone."

It's true that all the computers I've used here have very limited uses. You can type essays, connect to your smart band to track your fitness, look at your timetable, or even face-call your friends, but I've never been able to find a way to access anything else.

"But *why* would the Collective cut themselves off from the internet? Isn't that a bit, well, crazy?"

The professor snorts. "You still think of the internet as a good thing?"

"It is, isn't it?"

The professor starts pacing around the room. "Could everyone stop what they're doing for a moment. We need to educate our newest student on the perils of the internet. Who can tell Jamie why Arcadia is an internet-free zone?"

"It's partly for our security," offers Kalisha, one of the quieter girls. "No one out there knows that this place exists. We want to keep it that way and no one can hack into our system if we're not connected."

This is bad. This is really bad.

If what she's saying is true, then my mission is a waste of time. Even if I can gain access to the

Collective network, I won't be able to patch in a remote connection so the Resistance can get the information they need.

"It's also for protection from inside stupidity," says Tyler. "Someone in the Collective might want to invite a family member or friend from the outside world to join us here in Arcadia. If everyone did that, we'd be swamped with needy people. And we wouldn't want that, now would we? We know what outsiders are like."

There are a few sniggers. He's making a dig at my expense, as the new arrival.

However, his comment reminds me of something. My 'uncle' had been able to e-mail me from this place, so there must be *some* contact with the outside world.

So why would they lie? How come Aaron Greaves still has access to the internet if no one else does?

"It's also to protect our intellectual integrity," adds Freya. "The internet was meant to give us access to a wealth of information. You could find out anything from it. That was the theory. But, in practice, it turned out our brains simply couldn't cope with sorting out the facts from the fiction.

People became more stupid. The wealth of misinformation drowned out the true and factual information. Opinion triumphed over truth."

"I never thought of it that way before," I admit.

The professor looks around the room. "And there's one other reason we don't allow people to access the internet. Possibly the most important one. Anyone care to fill us in?"

The class look back at him, blankly.

"The internet wastes our time and steals our creativity. People were hooked on video games and social media feeds. They were getting less fit and less able to socialise every day. Everyone spent their time watching pointless videos, their phones and tablets sucking their lives away. They weren't happy, just distracted. And that meant people ceased to use their imaginations and creative abilities. They didn't want to learn new skills or exercise. No one read books. Their attention spans were tiny. It had to stop."

I feel myself blushing as I think about the amount of time I used to spend gaming. "Is that why there are no TVs or consoles in Arcadia either?"

"Exactly," he replies. "We need to control

technology, and make sure that whatever we let loose makes us into better, fitter human beings, not depressed, unfit morons."

"Like you, Jamie," says Tyler, and a few others laugh. The professor gives him a warning look, and he shuts up instantly.

I have so many questions, I don't know which to ask first. "But if computers are so bad, why do we still use them, and why learn so much about them?"

"Because computers are useful tools, like all technology, as long as you're careful about *how* you use them. And we have to master the use of computers in order to save the world."

There it is again.

Something has been bothering me about Arcadia ever since I arrived. Aaron Greaves has hinted at it more than once. And the professor makes vague references to it as well. I understand that Arcadia is meant to be this idyllic and utopian place, where we try to live healthy and productive lives and care for the environment. But when I first arrived, I always assumed it was a selfish or escapist dream; that these people couldn't care less about those who lived beyond the fence.

Now, though, I realise that isn't true. Everyone here believes they are working for the common good. They think that the choices we make here in Arcadia will affect those who live in the real world as well.

And the thing is, they're not stupid. But it doesn't make sense. These are the people who have developed a vaccine and kept it from everyone else. How can they justify that?

I open my mouth to ask something else, but the professor cuts me off.

"That's enough questions for now, Jamie. Keep working on your code."

"Yes, sir." I turn back to my screen and pretend to study its contents. But my mind is going crazy.

I'm beginning to wonder if the Collective are right, and the Resistance have got their wires crossed. Maybe the people in Arcadia aren't as evil as they think?

Is it possible that the Collective have a plan to save everyone else?

And what if I mess it up, by hacking into their network?

The longer I spend in this place, the more questions I have.

And the more I wonder if I'm on the right side.

Stop it, Zac.

I'm overthinking everything. I have a mission and I need to complete it. That's what I signed up for, as a member of the Resistance.

And that's what I'm going to do.

EIGHT

"Have you ever even rowed before?" Tyler sits behind me as I tug on the oars. I try to ignore him, but it's hard when someone keeps kicking you in the back.

When I'd climbed into the boat, I hadn't paid much attention to who took the seat behind me. That was a mistake. Now that we're on the water, it's too late to do anything about it.

He's not the only other person on board. Our class has been split into two teams and we're racing each other across the lake.

Ahmid is shouting instructions and encouragement, but it's hard to not be annoyed at him as he somehow got chosen as the coxswain. He's sat facing us, rather than putting in any of the hard graft.

"No wonder we're losing," mutters Tyler, as the other boat glides past. "You've got the muscles of a seven-year-old. When did you last work out?"

I feel myself going red. The skintight clothing emphasises my skinny build, and I'm fully aware that everyone else seems to have more muscles than me. Rowing is hard work, and sweat streams down my face as I move my arms in the smooth motion we've been taught. "Well, you've got the brains of a four-year-old but I'm not complaining."

"Yeah? Want to say that again?" I feel a big glob of spit hit me on the neck.

I try to pretend it doesn't bother me. "Pack it in. I'm trying to concentrate."

"Yeah? Make me!" He spits again, then kicks me hard in the ribs.

I let go of the oars and twist round in my seat to face him. "Will you–"

Before I can say another word, Tyler swings his leg, throwing me off balance. I tumble overboard, hitting the water with a loud splash. I sink some way before I manage to right myself and come up for air, coughing and spluttering.

Ahmid orders everyone to stop rowing. The boat is only a short distance away. But it's Tyler who's closest. He lifts one of his oars out of the rowlock and holds it out, as if he's offering a lifeline.

"Grab this," he yells, so everyone can hear.

I swim towards it, but as I reach out, he jabs me viciously in the chest. It knocks the wind out of me, making me gasp for air. I try to yell at him, but just get a mouthful of water which makes me cough some more.

"Nearly," he says, encouragingly. "You're nearly there. Try again!"

To everyone else, it looks like he's doing everything he can to help. But as I try to grip the oar, he makes another short, sudden movement, this time smacking it into my face, just below the eye. I yell out, rubbing my cheek as I tread water.

"Jamie, take the oar!" he yells, as if I'm being slow for not playing my part.

There isn't much else I can do. Fortunately, this time, he lets me take hold and pulls me towards the boat. When I get closer, he reaches down into the water and hauls me up, gripping the back of my tights.

"Are you ok?" he says, like we're mates.

I choke and splutter as I drop onto my seat, shivering in my wet clothes. I clutch my stomach and glare at him. "You did that deliberately!"

"Still sure you're not scared of me?" he sneers, under his breath. "Because I'm just getting started."

I've never been someone who likes fights. Being small for my age, it never ends well. Back at the Resistance base, Kieran used to tease me for being a doormat and letting everyone boss me around.

But something in Tyler's tone makes me snap. I shoot forward and start punching him in the face. Surprisingly, he doesn't fight back.

"Help! Get him off," he cries, as he leans away from my assault.

A boy called Kyle grabs me firmly from behind, getting me in an armlock. I wonder if he's going to throw me back in the water, but instead he holds me tight.

"Let me go." I struggle for freedom, but it's no use.

"What's happening over there?" yells the coach from the shore.

"Jamie's gone psycho!" shouts back Kyle.

"That's not–"

Kyle pushes my arm behind my back, making me cry out in pain.

"Come straight back to shore!" orders the coach.

Kyle keeps hold of me while the rest of our crew row us towards the small jetty. Tyler watches me the whole way, smirking. "Sure you don't want to do my run?"

"Screw you."

Once we've docked, the coach walks over, her face like thunder. Kyle forces me out of the boat, still gripping me tight. Tyler steps gingerly on to the jetty, his hand to his face.

"What happened?"

"Jamie went crazy," says Tyler, rubbing his cheek. "He said he was going to get me back for what happened in dodgeball earlier. He was about to start hitting me when he lost his balance and fell in the water."

"That's not true!"

"He looked like he couldn't swim all that well so I pulled him back into the boat with the oar," went on Tyler. "But as soon as he was on board he started lashing out. Fortunately, Kyle managed to get him under control."

The coach turns to me. "Well, Jamie, do you think you can control yourself now?"

I nod pathetically, water dripping from my hair and clothes.

"Let him go."

Kyle releases me and I rub my arm.

The coach puts her hands on her hips. "What do you have to say for yourself?"

"Tyler started it! He spat at me when we were in the boat, and kept kicking me in the back..."

Tyler shrugs. "He's lying. Why would I do that?"

The coach turns to Ahmid. "What did you see?"

"I didn't see anything," he admits, a bit embarrassed. "I was right at the other end of the boat. There were too many people in the way."

"I saw it," cuts in Kyle. "Jamie said something about how he was going to make Tyler pay and when I turned around, he was about to hit Ty in the face."

"I didn't mean to injure him when we played dodgeball," adds Tyler. "It was just an accident."

I turn on him. "You knew exactly what you were doing."

It's the wrong thing to say and the coach cuts me off. "So, it's true you were holding a grudge, and you thought you'd get your own back? Well things don't work that way here, Jamie. I know you're new, but we don't tolerate fighting."

"But Tyler was the one who…"

"Enough! I saw you hitting Tyler myself."

I stare at her, defiant.

"I don't think you should be too harsh, Coach," says Tyler, a mischievous glint in his eye. "Jamie's only been here a few weeks. It takes time to adjust. I don't know why he hates me so much, but I think if we had a bit more time to get to know one another, we could be good friends."

"I'll never be friends with you!" I spit out the words, furious.

Again, it's exactly what he wants. He's made it look like he has the moral high ground, and I've come across like a childish brat.

"Jamie, you will report to me at the end of lessons," snaps the coach. "We'll find a way to make you a little less keen on using your fists. Go and get changed. There are some dry clothes in the sports centre."

Tyler's mouth curls in triumph as I trudge past, my trainers squelching. "If you change your mind, just let me know."

That's not about his offer of friendship, and both of us know it. He's reminding me that until I fall into line, he's going to keep doing stuff like this.

And there's nothing I can do to stop him.

NINE

"You asked to see me, Coach."

"Ah, Jamie. Come in."

The gym is clean and bright, full of weight-lifting equipment. Like most of the buildings in Arcadia, two of the walls are made of glass, looking out on the forest.

"Step over here." The coach leads me to the corner where a large punchbag hangs from the ceiling. Next to it is a small screen in the wall. She presses a few buttons, then turns to face me. "You know what you did wrong today?"

Yeah, I stood up for myself.

There's no point arguing. It'll only make things worse.

"I punched Tyler."

"And you understand why that was a

mistake?"

"Because violence doesn't solve anything."

She nods. "We don't tolerate any form of violence in Arcadia, so if students lash out, there are consequences. By the time you finish here today, you're never going to want to punch anything again. Do you understand?"

"Yes, Coach."

"Good. Now hit the bag."

I ball up my fist and smack it hard.

A large number appears on the screen: 76.

In the bottom corner are two smaller numbers: 0/50.

"Harder," she says. "As hard as you can."

This time I punch it with all my might. The number 92 appears. The numbers in the corner change, too. They now read 1/50.

"That's good," says the coach. "You'll need to score over 90 for a punch to count, so you have to hit the bag with a lot of force to achieve that. Once you've done that fifty times, you can go. Your score is on the screen."

"But that'll take forever."

"Maybe you'll think twice before you hit anyone else."

I punch the bag again, but this time only score 82.

"It's impossible," I complain. "I'll never get fifty!"

"If you're going to whine, I'll make it sixty. Want me to do that?"

"No, Coach."

"You sure?"

"Yes, Coach."

"I'm leaving now, but I will be checking on your progress remotely, and you don't even want to know what will happen if you try to cheat or if you leave before you're done."

I gulp and take another swing at the bag. It scores 90 dead-on. Only forty-eight more punches like that and I can go home.

The coach heads out of the gym without a backward glance. As soon as she's gone, I pummel the bag, hoping that if I let loose with all my rage and anger, I might make a dent in the target. Sadly, after a torrent of punches, only a couple count towards my score.

I'm already slick with sweat and my right arm is aching.

Slow and steady, Zac.

I wait a while before I try again.

That works. I find that if I take a brief rest between each punch, I can just about make them hard enough to register above 90.

Even using that method, by the time I only have twenty punches left, I'm exhausted. I drop to the floor, panting.

Someone knocks on the window and I glance over to see Tyler, Jack and Kyle laughing and pointing. Kyle does an impression of someone swinging their fist and then falling over.

I force myself back on my feet, trying to channel my anger and annoyance into my fists. By the time I've scored another six, my audience have gone. Watching me must have lost some of its entertainment value.

I keep slogging away, taking time to rest between each couple of strikes, gradually whittling down the total.

The last three points are a killer. I can barely lift my arm, let alone hit with enough force for it to count. I try using my left arm instead, but it's not strong enough.

Summoning the last of my energy, I somehow do it. I take a couple of desperate swings, throwing my entire weight behind them.

The counter reads 50/50.

I can finally leave.

After a large swig of water from the drinking fountain, I head out the door.

***

I'm feeling sorry for myself as I trudge up the ramp to the tree house. It's been a long day and I still haven't done my 5k run or started on any homework. Added to that, I stink: a potent mix of lake-water and boy-sweat.

I must look a state as I slouch into the kitchen.

Maddie looks up, concerned. "What happened to you?"

"I had to stay behind." I drop into a chair. "Any chance of one of those awesome energy drinks?"

"No chance." That's not Maddie's voice. It's my uncle's. He strides in, furious. "I heard what happened on the lake today."

"I bet you didn't get the full story," I mutter.

"You punched a boy. Tyler DeBronte."

"Yeah," I admit. "But he deserved it."

Aaron Greaves sits down opposite me and

gives an exasperated sigh. "Physical violence is always wrong. How are we ever going to solve the world's problems if we keep hitting each other?"

There it is again.

Much as I want to set the record straight about what Tyler did, my frustration boils over. "Solving the world's problems? Is that what you think you do here? Cause all I've seen is you trying to create your perfect little society in the woods while everyone else is miserable in lockdown. How can you lecture me about the way I treat others when you're responsible for that?"

Aaron shakes his head. "You wouldn't understand."

I try to keep my voice even. "What? That you have a vaccine for Vicron-X but that you won't release it because you're too selfish. You're right. I don't get it. How could anyone be so evil? Do you know what it's actually like in the real world? People are dying from the virus. No one can leave their houses. Life is horrible out there."

Maddie lays some food on the table, looking awkward. Some kind of lentil dish with rice. It doesn't make me feel any better.

Aaron picks up a fork and takes a mouthful,

chewing slowly. "You're way out of line."

"Who cares? On the moral scale, how does answering back compare to keeping a nation in lockdown? I'll go to my room, shall I? Or do some extra chores? What punishment do *you* get for what *you're* doing? Answer me that."

Aaron looks at me as if I'm stupid. "I thought you'd have worked it out by now, Jamie."

"Worked what out?"

"We're trying to save the world."

TEN

He's so confident, so self-assured.

How can he believe that?

"How?" I say. "How does keeping everyone in lockdown save anything?"

"Ever heard of the climate crisis?" Aaron raises his eyebrows as he takes a sip of his water.

I still haven't touched my food. I pick up a fork and move it aimlessly around the plate. "What's that got to do with it?"

"A few years ago, things were spiralling out of control. The planet was in chaos. Governments seemed powerless to stop our insane journey towards self-destruction. Businesses didn't care; not if it hurt their profits. And people? Well, people are selfish and contradictory. Most of them, anyway."

Yeah, like you.

I take a small forkful of the rice. It tastes as bad as it looks. I can feel my heart thudding faster than normal. I feel like I'm on the verge of some kind of breakthrough and I don't want to interrupt.

"All it would take is a two degree rise in global temperature until we hit the point of no return. You know what happens then?"

I try to remember. "The ice caps melt?"

"That's right. And that makes things exponentially worse. One disaster leads to another, like a snowball rolling down a hill, picking up speed and getting bigger as it goes."

"I still don't see what this has to do with the vaccine," I say, stubbornly.

"Nothing could stop us destroying the planet. Humans, I mean. Not until Vicron-X came along. Then, the world went into lockdown, one country at a time. In a few short months, our carbon emissions dropped dramatically. For the first time in living memory, there was hope."

I drop my fork and stare at him. "You don't mean…"

"Yes, Vicron-X gave us an opportunity to stop

the clock, to get time to think and plan, to come up with strategies to save the planet, to reset our society. In many ways, it was the best thing that could have happened."

"Tell that to the people who died."

Aaron pauses and looks at me. "That was unfortunate. No one could do anything about that."

"But now you can. Now, you have the vaccine."

"Have you stopped to think about what will happen when everyone gets it? When no one is worried about Vicron-X any more?"

"Life will return to normal, I guess."

"Exactly. And in a few short years, even more people will die in natural catastrophes due to climate change. Half the world will starve. Is that what you want?"

I shift awkwardly in my seat. "No. Of course not. But you can't keep everyone in lockdown forever."

Aaron looks away. "It won't be forever."

"How long then?"

"Just until we can find solutions. Every day, we work on fresh problems, think about new possibilities. We have some of the best minds in the country here in Arcadia. Together, we can make a difference. We can change the world."

I stare at him, wondering if he's a genius or a madman. His explanation seems genuine. It explains everything about this place, from the obsession with the environment to the constant ethical debates in the classroom.

"How close are you? To finding solutions, I mean?"

Aaron looks uncomfortable. "There's so much to think about. We're going as fast as we can, but it takes time."

"Is that where you go every day? To work on solutions?"

He nods. "We're trying to ensure that we can get everything in place, to make sure that when the vaccine is released, people live differently."

"And that's why you're hacking into people's computers, to ensure that you can get everything organised in the outside world." As soon as I've said it, I regret it. How would I know that? That's something the Resistance told me, not something anyone has revealed in Arcadia.

Aaron looks up sharply. "How do you know about that?"

I think fast. If I don't give a decent answer, my cover is blown. "I figured it out, from the way you rescued me and brought me here. And it also explains why we spend so long programming in class."

He seems to relax. "You're a bright boy, Jamie. Too bright to get caught brawling with the likes of Tyler DeBronte."

I've calmed down now. All my energy is spent. "Well, for what it's worth, after what Coach made me do, I won't be hitting anything else for weeks."

That makes him smile. "I'm glad to hear it."

I casually play with my food, wondering how much more I can find out. "The professor said something in class that confused me."

"What's that?"

"He said the network here in Arcadia isn't connected to the internet. But that can't be true, because you were able to contact me when I was on the outside."

He examines me closely. I don't think he's going to say anything, but he does. "I guess I can tell you: there are two networks. The main one is disconnected from the outside world. That's what you use for school and at home. But the computers inside the Nexus are different."

"The Nexus? Where you go to work every day?"

"That's right. That's where the action happens."

From the outside, the Nexus is the biggest building in the red zone. It's a tower of glass and steel on the edge of the lake. If I could get inside, then I might be able to complete my mission for the Resistance.

I decide to push my luck. "Can I see it sometime? Inside, I mean?"

"Why would you want to do that?"

I give a casual shrug. "Just interested, I guess."

"Maybe. We'll see. Did you have any thoughts on what you wanted to do this weekend?"

I feel a little guilty that I haven't checked with him before making plans. "Ahmid and Freya invited me to go camping with them. Is that ok?"

"As long as you stay out of trouble."

"I will. I promise."

After that, we eat in silence. That suits me fine. I have a lot to think about and a lot to accomplish.

First, I need to find that copy-token. Then, I have to persuade my uncle to give me access to the Nexus so I can plant it on their network and get the Resistance the information they need.

Somehow, I need to do all that without raising suspicion or getting caught.

And I need to do it soon.

ELEVEN

Friday drags.

I keep looking out the windows, desperate to escape the classroom. It's dry and sunny, the perfect weather for camping. I can't wait to get out there, and to hunt for the fake stone.

When the professor finally releases us for the weekend, I bolt out the door, then have to wait for Ahmid and Freya to catch up.

"What's the hurry?" asks Ahmid, grinning. "Anyone would think you were keen to get away."

"I am. It's been a long week." That much was true. Tyler hadn't been brazen enough to attack me again, but he did keep muttering threats and insults, and I was tired of his sniping. "A relaxing weekend in the woods sounds like heaven."

"We'll have to do our homework when we get

back," points out Freya.

I couldn't care less about that. I'm worried that something will stop us from going. "I hope everything's where we left it."

Ahmid looks at me in surprise. "Why wouldn't it be?"

"Someone might have taken it."

He laughs. "It's not like that here. We don't have thieves in Arcadia. Besides, there are loads more tents and stuff in the communal supplies if anyone wants them."

"I guess."

He's right. When we enter the supplies cabin, the camping equipment is still piled in the corner. We pack the rucksacks carefully, then haul them on to our shoulders. Mine isn't as heavy as I feared and the padded straps help a lot.

"Ok, let's go," I say, eager to be off.

I lead them along the path that will take us to the stream. It's not long before we're walking past the boundary flags of the red circle and out into the woods.

"What's the point of the flags?" I ask. "I mean, we're allowed to cross them, so why mark out the red zone at all?"

"It's to protect against infection," says Ahmid.

"But we've all had the vaccine."

"Yeah, for Vicron-X. But what if it mutates and the vaccine no longer works? Or a different virus comes along? Arcadia is built on the principle that if we separate society into zones, then we won't need to lock everyone down in their houses again. We'd just need to isolate the zones."

"So, everyone lives and works in their own zone?"

"That's the plan."

"While there's no risk, we're allowed in the other zones," adds Freya. "Sometimes there are competitions or social events, or you might just want to visit people. That's allowed, but we're careful that we don't get dependent on each other."

"The other zones are all spread at different points around the lake," says Ahmid.

"I've seen them. From my bedroom, I can see over the lake and there's a cluster of buildings on the shore opposite."

"That's probably the yellow zone. They're closest."

We shut up for a bit after that, enjoying the sounds of the forest. The sun beats down and I can feel sweat on my back. We have a few hours until dusk, plenty of time to reach our destination and set up camp before it gets dark.

"Which way?" asks Ahmid, as we come to a fork in the path.

"To the right," I say confidently. I've been down this path enough times.

"Is it much further?" asks Freya.

"Not too far. Maybe a mile from here. But it's worth it."

"I'm hungry," moans Ahmid. "What do we have to eat?"

"You're not having anything yet," snaps Freya. "You wouldn't normally eat this early."

"But we've walked for miles."

I laugh at him. "We haven't come that far. It's only been an hour."

"This bag is heavy."

Freya turns to me, an amused expression on her face. "You'll have to excuse Ahmid. He's not exactly the outdoors type."

"I figured."

It doesn't really matter. It's not long before we

come to the clearing. It's at the base of a small valley, not far from the boundary fence. Wooded slopes rise on either side of a fast-moving stream. Next to it is a flat grassy stretch of land—the perfect place to put our tents.

"It's beautiful!" declares Freya.

"I told you. Our own private resort."

***

"I just can't figure this out," admits Ahmid, looking at the crumpled instructions. "It says we're meant to put poles in an X shape across the whole tent, but there's only one pole."

"Check again in the bag," says Freya.

I pick it up and rummage around, but it's clear there aren't any others in there.

"Someone must have lost one when they last used it."

Ahmid shook his head. "It must be somewhere."

We check the ground and stretch out the flysheet to see if the pole has got caught up in it, but there's no sign of it.

Freya groans. "What do we do now? Do we

have to call the whole thing off?"

I can't let that happen. Not when we've got this close to properly searching for the copy-token. "It's a dry night. We can sleep outside, under the stars."

Ahmid looks uncertain. "I'm not sure that's a good idea. Is it safe?"

"It's an adventure. Come on, it'll be fun."

Thankfully, Freya agrees. "He's right. We can't let one minor problem ruin our weekend."

"If you're sure." Ahmid looks distinctly uncomfortable at the idea of sleeping in the open air, but he doesn't have the energy to argue.

I nudge him playfully. "I know what'll cheer you up. Let's have something to eat."

***

We tuck into our provisions, and Ahmid starts to relax.

"Glad we came now?" I ask.

"I guess," he admits.

I stand up and stretch. "I'm going down to the stream, before the sun goes down."

"I'll come with you," says Freya.

We wander down to the water and jump between rocks, seeing who can jump the furthest without falling in. It isn't long before Ahmid joins us.

After a while, I start looking for stones, trying to remember the exact shape and size of the one the Resistance had showed me they would hide the device inside. I know it has to be around here somewhere.

I survey the mass of stones on the stream bed and try not to despair.

You can do this, Zac.

"What are you looking for?" asks Freya.

I'm prepared for that and have an excuse ready. "I need stones, to build a stone balance sculpture. They have to be the right size though—like this." I show her the stone I'm holding.

"What's a stone balance sculpture?" asks Ahmid, confused.

"You build a tower of stones in the middle of a stream and you see how high you can make it. They're pretty amazing."

"What's the point?"

"It's just for fun."

He shrugs, as if he'll never understand that.

But, even if he thinks I'm weird, he helps to hunt for stones. So does Freya. Before long, there's a large pile by the side of the stream. I search through it, pulling out stones that look like they could be the one I'm looking for, but sadly they're all real.

"Surely that's enough?" asks Ahmid at last, sitting down on the bank.

"I guess." I look at the pile of useless stones.

Freya sits down next to him. "Aren't you going to start building?"

"Sure."

I pick up the largest rock from the pile and make my way to the stream, trying to look more confident than I feel. I bend down to create a base for the sculpture in a shallow part of the stream. Once it's in place, I return to the pile and select a couple of other large stones.

Freya and Ahmid are watching with interest as I try to balance them on the foundation I just laid.

The inevitable happens. I can't get them to stay on top of each other and one plops into the water. I quickly retrieve it and try again but making these things balance is harder than it looks.

"Do you actually know what you're doing?" asks Freya.

I shrug, trying to appear like it's no big deal. "Sort of. I haven't done it for a while. I'm not an expert or anything. I think I might wait until tomorrow to properly have a go."

I step back across some stones to the grassy bank, leaving my feeble first attempts behind me. By now, the sun has disappeared behind the hill and the sky is getting darker. There's a slight chill in the air as we arrange our roll mats on the flattest part of the ground. We lay the sleeping bags neatly on top.

When I turn around, Ahmid is waving his hands wildly in front of his face.

"You ok?"

"It's the midges," he whines. "We're being attacked."

He's right. In the dusky light I can see clouds of them forming around my head. I start to itch; I'm not sure if they're biting me or if I'm just being paranoid. Still, I can't let these bugs ruin my only opportunity to find the copy-token. "They're just flies. Ignore them."

He's not going to let the matter drop that easily. "I don't see how we can sleep here with these things biting our faces off."

Freya frowns. "Ahmid's right. We won't be able to sleep without protection. But I think we could put up the inner part of the tent like a mosquito net if we can hang it from a low branch. Then we can sleep inside."

I could kiss her for coming up with a solution. "Let's do it."

We set to work, busying ourselves with attaching the inner-tent to one of the trees. It takes a while to find the best way to support it, but we eventually make it work. The pole is bent at a weird angle and the fabric is being pulled in strange directions, but I'm not complaining. It's going to rescue us from being eaten alive by midges and save our weekend.

We drag the roll mats and sleeping bags inside our makeshift shelter. We're going to be able to spend the night out here after all.

At least, that's what we think.

TWELVE

The forest is dark and eerie as I stand next to a tree, relieving myself.

Ahmid is a short distance away, doing the same. "It's pretty creepy out here," he says.

I finish my business and pull up my tights. "I'm heading back to the tent."

"Wait for me," he pleads.

I can sense the fear in his voice. "I can't. There's this enormous monster heading this way, and it looks hungry. I think it's going to get whichever of us is the slowest."

"You're such an idiot," he complains, "but if you want a race, then I'll give you one. First one in their sleeping bag gets the last chocolate bar!"

He dashes past before I've even taken in what he's said, but I catch him up. I rugby-tackle him onto the grass before scrambling up and racing ahead.

"You're such a cheat," he shouts after me.

I kick off my shoes as I enter, then slip inside my sleeping bag, laughing. "Do I get that chocolate bar now?"

But I don't laugh for long. Something is soaking through my top and tights. I unzip the sleeping bag and realise all too late what's happened. Someone has gunged it with something horrible. It looks like black treacle. I climb to my feet, sticky strands hanging off me.

"What the hell? Which one of you did this? That's going too far!"

Ahmid looks as surprised as me as he enters the tent. "I didn't! I wouldn't do that!"

I can hear Freya approaching, heading back over from the nearby trees.

"Frey, did you do anything to Jamie's sleeping bag?" calls Ahmid. "It's full of gunk."

"No way."

I step out of the tent covered in black, sticky goo. As I lift my arms away from my body, I feel like I've been smeared in glue. "This is gross."

"Can't you wash it off in the stream,"

suggested Freya.

"It's too cold now." There's no way I'll dry off if I get my clothes that wet. I'd rather deal with the gunge than freeze to death.

"Uh oh," says Ahmid. "The other two sleeping bags are the same. They've all been sabotaged. This camping trip is turning into a complete disaster."

"It must be Tyler," I say, bitterly. "He heard we were going camping when the professor asked what we were doing this weekend."

Ahmid steps out of the shelter. "I can't believe he's done this."

"We don't have any proof," notes Freya.

"But who else would have done it?" She holds up her hands. "I know it was him. You know it was him. All I'm saying is we can't prove it. And he knows that."

The midges and mosquitoes are buzzing around me in a cloud, seemingly even more attracted to me now I'm covered in treacle. I wave my arms to try to ward them off but it's useless.

"What do we do?"

I know the answer, even though I don't want

to hear it.

"We have to go back," says Ahmid. "We can't stay here now. Not without sleeping bags and with you in that state."

"I agree," said Freya. "We tried our best, but it's time to give up."

Much as I want to press on and find the stone, even I can't sleep in these conditions. I just want to get home and get clean, back to a warm bed.

"Ok," I sigh. "I think you're right."

I was all for leaving the shelter and the ruined sleeping bags by the stream, but Freya and Ahmid were horrified that I'd even suggest it.

"That's the kind of thing that ruins the planet!" exclaims Freya. "Leaving junk around in beautiful places like this."

"And if you even drop litter in Arcadia, you get in serious trouble," adds Ahmid.

We stuff the sleeping bags back into the small bags they came in, roll up the mats and take down the shelter. It's not easy doing all of that in the dark, but Ahmid holds a light for us while me and Freya do most of the work.

It's pitch-black by the time we're wandering back through the woods, the heavy packs on our shoulders. I try to ignore the sticky sensation that I feel every time one part of my body makes contact with another. I hate it. This is worse than any of the pranks Kieran pulled on me when we were in the Resistance. And there's a vast difference between being pranked by a mate and sabotaged by an enemy.

Without a doubt, Tyler has won this round. He's also wrecked my chances of finding the fake stone anytime soon. I doubt Ahmid and Freya will ever want to camp again.

The walk back seems to take an age. We trudge along, not speaking. We've been defeated and we know it.

"You ok?" asks Freya, gently, as I scuff my trainers in the dirt.

"I guess." I run a hand through my hair and instantly regret it as I feel some of the stickiness get caught up in it. "Well, I've been better, obviously. But I don't want Tyler to get away with this."

"Neither do I," she agrees. "But there's not a lot we can do."

"We should have checked everything more carefully before we set off," points out Ahmid.

I snort. "What happened to 'people in Arcadia respect other people's stuff' and all that?"

Ahmid goes quiet for a moment before he replies. "It's never happened before. Tyler really doesn't like you. He went to a special effort for this."

"If someone had caught him doing it, he'd have been in serious trouble," agrees Freya. "Now we know he's raised his game, we need to take extra precautions."

"I just wish he'd leave me alone."

But as we make our way past the red boundary, I know that's never going to happen.

Not unless I give in to his demands.

THIRTEEN

Something isn't right.

From outside the tree house, I can hear raised voices, but I can't make out the words.

Ahmid and Freya have headed to their own homes, and I've made my way back up the ramp to my cabin.

I hesitate by the front door, wondering if I'm about to interrupt my uncle at a bad time.

Should I go inside?

It's my home, after all. It's not my fault the camping trip has been abandoned.

I quietly open the door and creep down the corridor. The voices are coming from the kitchen. The door is ajar, but only a little, and they can't see me as I make my way to my bedroom.

"You have to see sense, Aaron. We can't carry

on like this."

"I refuse to give up." That's my uncle's voice. "Arcadia is meant to be a place of hope."

"It is. It will be. From here, we will rebuild the country, slowly and surely, caring for the planet as we go."

"After we let everyone else die? It's not a serious solution. I won't entertain it."

My blood runs cold. I stand frozen to the spot, my heart thudding.

"It's not ideal, I grant you. But it's the only way forward. Otherwise, we *all* die, along with the planet."

"Not ideal?" explodes Aaron. "You're talking about mass murder."

"I'm talking about survival of the fittest. It's nature's way."

I hear someone slam down a glass. "If we just had more time, we could change society. We've already put in so much work."

"But we don't. The people out there are getting restless. It's becoming harder and harder to suppress the truth and explain why we still haven't got a vaccine. Ever since we had to quell the Resistance, things have got worse. People aren't as afraid of the virus as they used to be. If we don't act soon, we'll lose control."

"But what you're suggesting… it's evil…"

"It's the only rational thing to do. Fewer people will die this way."

"I won't allow it."

"You may not have any choice. I've called an assembly. We're putting it to the vote."

"You can't."

"Get with the plan, or I'll have you removed."

"You overestimate your power, Eugene," warns Aaron.

"We'll see."

Without warning, the kitchen door swings open. The man standing there is even taller than my uncle. He has black hair and a stern face. His expression changes to one of shock when he sees me.

"What are you doing here, boy?" He grabs hold of my top and drags me towards him.

"I just got back," I mutter. "I was going to my room."

"What did you hear?"

"Nothing," I lie. "Nothing at all."

"Let my nephew go," orders my uncle.

"Gladly." The man releases me so fast, I fall to the floor, then wipes his sticky hand on a wall. "It's over, Aaron. Don't fight me on this or you'll regret it."

He storms out, slamming the door behind him.

My uncle looks down at me. "I thought you went camping."

I climb slowly to my feet. "Someone sabotaged our stuff. They stole a pole out of the tent and gunged the sleeping bags. I think it must have been Tyler."

He allows himself a wry smile. "I wish that's all I had to worry about." A brief pause. "What *did* you hear?"

"There was a lot of shouting. He said something about calling an assembly, and that you needed to back him or you'd regret it. It sounded serious."

"It is serious, but I'll handle it. You better get yourself cleaned up."

He's not wrong. I slip gratefully into my room and strip off the sticky clothes.

I'm starting to see why my uncle looks so stressed all the time. Things in Arcadia are not as perfect as they seem.

But why did he accuse Eugene of planning mass murder? Surely, he didn't mean they were going to wipe out the rest of the population?

If that's true, then it makes my mission for the Resistance more important than ever. I have to find that copy-token, and get access to the Nexus. If I don't get it done soon, everyone could die.

But finding the fake stone is like hunting for a needle in a haystack. There's no way to do it. I'd need a metal detector to stand any chance at all. And I'm not likely to find one of those just sitting around.

Or am I?

The communal supplies cabin!

That had shelves stacked with random gear and equipment. What if there's one in there?

From what I saw, Freya and Ahmid just chose whatever they wanted from the shelves and signed it out on a list. Maybe I could do the same?

As I step under the hot water and wash off the treacle, I feel a new sense of hope. With a metal detector, it will be so much easier to find what I'm looking for. Maybe I can still succeed in my mission.

First thing tomorrow, I plan to check the place out and see if it has what I need.

FOURTEEN

"We're out of soya milk."

I bang the bowl on the kitchen surface. "You could have told me *before* I poured out the muesli."

Aaron looks up at me. "Less of the attitude. I've got enough on my plate without dealing with whiny teenagers."

"Sorry."

"As it's Maddie's day off today, you can fetch some from the store."

What did your last slave die of?

"Do we need anything else?"

"Not that I'm aware of." He puts down his tablet for a moment, giving me his full attention. "About last night, you're not going to tell anyone what you heard, are you?"

I shrug and take a raisin from my bowl. "Of course not. None of my business."

"There's a red zone gathering this evening. Now that camping is off the cards, I'm guessing you'll join me?"

"Can't see why not. But what is it, exactly?"

"Just an opportunity for everyone to get together and have fun. Like a party on the lakeshore. Live music, good food, that sort of thing."

"Sounds awesome."

"It is." He turns his attention back to his tablet. "Now, go fetch the milk."

"Sure." I resist the temptation to salute as I grab a large empty bottle and head for the door. I don't want to get grounded, or given more jobs to do, just because he's annoyed.

If all goes to plan, I have the whole day to try to get hold of a metal detector and head into the woods. It's my best chance to get the mission back on track.

No stupid mistakes, Zac.

I can't afford to mess this up.

***

It's not far to the place where everyone gets their food and drink. It doesn't look like much; just another large log cabin. I've only been here once before, when Maddie asked me to fetch some rice. The door creaks as I walk in.

"Young Master Jamie, if I'm not mistaken." The store-keeper peers at me over the top of her spectacles.

"Yeah, that's right. Hi."

"What are you looking for today?"

The store isn't like a supermarket back home. For one thing, you don't have to pay for anything. Everything is free; you just take what you want. Crazy, right?

The other thing that makes it different is the fact that nothing comes pre-packaged. Everything is stored in giant containers and you have to scoop or pour it out into your own tubs and bottles.

"We're out of soya milk." I hold up the empty bottle.

She hobbles over and inspects the receptacle. "Doesn't look like you've cleaned that out."

"I didn't."

She shakes her head. "No good putting fresh milk in a dirty bottle. It'll be full of bacteria."

"Good to know." I glance around. "Is there anywhere I can wash it?"

"Sink's through there." She points to a door behind the counter.

"Thanks." I wander through to the back room, where there's a huge stainless-steel sink. It reminds me of when I used to do the washing up in the pub that doubled as the Resistance headquarters. Just thinking about the place makes me homesick. I wonder whether they've given up on me, or whether they're still waiting for me to complete my mission and return.

The woman is standing right behind me. "Make sure you rinse it well."

"I'll do my best." I can't help thinking how much simpler everything was when I used to just buy ordinary milk in a plastic bottle. After a while, I hold up the container. "Will that do?"

"Once it's been sterilized." She takes it off me and puts it in something that looks like a giant microwave. It lights up when she presses a button. "This kills any remaining germs."

Just how complicated can it be to get some

milk?

Finally, she opens the door and takes out the bottle. "Now it's ready."

We wander back through to the store, where she holds it under a tap and white liquid sloshes into the bottle. Once it's full, she puts on the lid and hands it over. "Do you need anything else?"

Yeah, a break from stupid chores.

"No, that's everything for now. Thanks."

At least I can now have my muesli. Then, I can get on with my mission.

***

"He'll be there at eleven." Uncle Aaron is speaking into his tablet as I step into the kitchen. He presses a button and looks over.

That doesn't sound good.

"I got the milk." I wonder whether to just dump the bottle in the fridge and leave before he can ruin my plans.

It's already too late.

"I just had a call from Helen, who's arranging tonight's gathering."

"Uh huh," I say. I can't rush off now, so I pour

the milk on my muesli. I might as well eat.

"She needs some help getting everything ready. I volunteered you for the job."

"But I have plans," I blurt out. "I'm busy today."

"What plans? You were meant to be camping."

Think fast, Zac.

"Ahmid invited me round to work on his robots. We chatted about it as we walked back last night. He'll be gutted if I don't go."

"That's ok. You have a couple of hours before Helen needs you."

"I promised him I'd be there all day."

"Call him and cancel. He'll get over it."

"But..."

Aaron slams down his mug. "This isn't a negotiation. You will do as you're told."

I crunch on the cereal, mutinous.

"I'm serious," he adds. "If I hear you've been anything other than helpful, I'll have you doing so much community service, you won't have time to breathe, you hear me?"

I can't contain my anger. "How is that different to what I'm doing right now? Fetch this, do that, finish this homework. Oh wait, that's not good enough, do it again."

"Fine, have it your way." He picks up the tablet and swipes at the screen. "I won't have you turning into a brat."

I gulp. "What are you doing?"

"I'm resetting the boundary conditions on your smart band. At eleven, you need to be at the jetty, where Helen will be setting everything up. I can't see any reason you'll need to wander more than eighty metres from there, so that's your perimeter. Cross the line, and I'll get an alert. And then things get really difficult for you, do you hear?"

I nod, miserably. "How long do I have to stay there?"

"Four hours should do it."

"Four hours?" I almost drop my bowl. "How much setting up is there?"

"No idea. But if you've finished before that, you can just sit on the lakeshore and reflect on your attitude."

This just gets worse.

Aaron stands up. "I'm heading off to work. Make sure you're at the jetty on time, else you'll regret it."

I give a curt nod.

As soon as he's gone, I spring into action. I dump the remaining muesli in the sink and dash out the door. Time is too precious to spend it eating. I have to get to the communal supplies shed to see if there's a metal detector. I need to know whether my plan will actually work.

Even with my uncle's boundaries, I'll still have *some* time.

And I plan to find that device.

Whatever it takes.

FIFTEEN

The supplies cabin is deserted. Shelves tower above me, full of random items and large plastic containers. The clipboard hangs on the wall, and I lift it off and flick through.

My eyes scan the list: Measuring tape... Mental health resources... Mouse traps...

Too far.

I'm starting to think it's not there, that my plan won't work.

Then, I spot what I'm looking for: Metal Detectors, F12.

Yes!

I dash to the right aisle and frantically search the shelf numbers for the location. Finally, I see it. There's only one metal detector, but that's all I need. When I pull it off the shelf, it weighs a lot less than I expect. But there's a rechargeable battery too, and a small instruction booklet. I suddenly realise a potential flaw in my plan. I click in the battery and flick on the switch. The detector turns on but a 'low power' LED also lights up. It needs to be charged.

It would, wouldn't it?

Flicking through the booklet, I discover that a full charge takes eight hours, and that gives enough power for two hours of use. That's good news, all things considered. If I plug it in now, it should be three-quarters charged by the time I'm allowed to leave the jetty.

Then, if I run fast to the stream, I should have at least an hour and a half to hunt for the device before I have to head back for tonight's event. It's going to be one hell of a day, but I can just about do it.

I locate a power socket on the wall and plug the device in.

"There you are." A man is striding towards me. "You're one of the kids that borrowed all the camping equipment."

"Yeah, that's allowed isn't it? I mean, Freya and Ahmid signed it out and everything."

"There was no problem with borrowing it. But you have to return things clean, ready for others to use." He grabs me by the arm.

"Hey, let go."

"You're coming with me. You've got some cleaning up to do."

I allow him to pull me out of the supplies cabin and round the back, where three sleeping bags lie open on the ground, covered in treacle.

I can feel my face burn. "It's not what it looks like. That wasn't us."

"Well your names are on the sheet. You're the only people who have used them for over a month."

"Someone sabotaged our stuff. When we got them out, they were already like that."

The man raises his eyebrows. "You want me to believe that for no reason at all, some random person just pulled out three sleeping bags and did this?"

I pull away from him. "Why would *we* do it? We were just trying to sleep in them? It's not like we'd want to gunge ourselves, is it?"

The man shrugs. "Some kind of dare. A prank war that got out of hand. I have no idea why you'd do it. But now, you need to sort it. If these aren't cleaned up by lunchtime, I'll put you on report. And you know what that means?"

I shake my head.

"You won't be allowed to borrow anything else from the stores, for a start. And your uncle will hear about it."

I can't let that happen. I need that metal detector.

"Fine. I'll clean the sleeping bags." I wonder if I should ask whether Freya and Ahmid are going to have to help, but I don't want to drop them in it. I guess I can do it myself.

"There was a pole missing from the tent as well."

"That wasn't our fault. It wasn't in the bag."

The man puts his hands on his hips. "Everything is checked when it's returned. The last people to use this tent had two poles. You kids take it and return it with one. Care to explain?"

"Someone stole it."

"The same person who wrecked the sleeping bags, I'm guessing?"

I nod, miserably.

"Well, replacing a pole for that exact tent isn't easy. I'll be putting the three of you on extra community service."

There's no point arguing. He'll never believe it wasn't us. "What should I use to wash the treacle off?"

"Get a bucket and cloth from inside the supplies cabin. Then go to the store and ask for a small amount of powder detergent and mix it with water. That should wash off the worst of it. Once you've taken off the excess, you'll need to take the bags to the launderette and put them through a machine."

"I'm on it." I stumble back inside and hunt for the bucket and cloth.

There goes the rest of my morning.

I'm either the unluckiest kid alive, or life in Arcadia is not all it's cracked up to be.

***

"Look who it is. Enjoy your camping trip?"

I turn around to see Tyler standing over me, smirking.

"Get lost, Tyler. You've had your fun." I scrub

furiously at the sleeping bag.

"You really should take better care of the equipment," he gloats. "Other people might want to use that, you know."

He's trying to get me to do something stupid, like hit him, but I'm not going to fall for it. "You ruined our weekend. And now I have to clean up the mess you made. I hope you're happy."

"As it happens, I am. But I also wanted to ask a favour." Tyler sits down on a log. "I'm meant to be running 8k today, but I don't feel like it."

"Yeah? Well it sucks to be you."

"I thought you might run it for me, if I lend you my smart band."

"I'd rather nail my testicles to a wall."

That makes him laugh. "I don't know if you're being brave or stupid, but until you start helping me, things are only going to get worse. I thought you'd have figured that out by now."

"Go swivel."

"If you're sure?" He leans over and looks at the bag. "Ew, that's nasty. I think you've missed a bit."

He spits at me, then walks off. That kid is winding me right up. But I can't get distracted.

Right now, I have much bigger things to worry about than Tyler LeBronte.

SIXTEEN

Ahmid is waiting by the jetty when I arrive. Clearly, he's also been roped in to helping set up for tonight's event.

"Had a nice relaxing morning?" I can't hide the annoyance from my voice.

"Not too bad. Why?"

"I've spent the last two hours cleaning treacle out of sleeping bags."

He looks shocked. "You're not serious?"

"This guy grabbed me and told me that if I didn't do it, there'd be consequences." I look out over the lake. "I could probably have got him to call your families too, but I didn't."

Ahmid puts his hand on my shoulder. "You're a proper mate. I'm sorry you got stuck with that. I didn't realise they'd check."

I can't stay cross at him; he's being too nice. "So, your parents decided to volunteer you for some slave labour as well?"

"The joys of being a teenager in Arcadia. It's not like we have rights."

That makes me snort with laughter. "That's what I tried to tell my uncle."

"Bet he loved that."

"You're not kidding."

"Are you boys here to help, or to stand around chatting?" A fierce-looking lady strides towards us from a nearby cabin.

"Help, I guess. What needs doing?"

"We need the big marquee carrying out from over there. We're going to set it up right here."

"The marquee?" Ahmid sounds surprised.

The woman brushes her hair from her eyes and stares up at the sky. "It's meant to rain this afternoon. Might even carry on this evening."

I glance around. We're standing on the shore of the lake. A wide grassy area separates the water from the start of the forest. There's almost no shelter.

"Wouldn't we be better to cancel? To postpone it to another night?"

"Why? A little rain never hurt anyone. Anyway, we can shelter under the marquee. Once you boys have helped me put it up."

"We're on it," says Ahmid, pulling me gently by the arm towards the large cabin on the lakeshore.

"Let me guess," I mutter. "That's Helen."

"The very same."

***

As I stare at the mass of poles and canvas, I can't help wondering if we'll have it up in four hours. I'm desperate to get away as fast as I can. As soon as my smart band will allow me to leave, I have to go hunting for the copy-token.

"I think we start by putting all the poles together," says Helen, rustling a large sheet of instructions. She's not filling me with confidence.

Ahmid is kneeling down, trying to sort them out. "If we get the poles into piles of the same length, then we should be able to work out what goes where."

"Sounds good." I crouch down to help.

"I'm not sure she knows what she's doing," he murmurs to me, so Helen can't hear.

I nudge him. "She's probably got the instructions upside down."

"Do you think she'd let us take a look at them?"

"Maybe."

It takes some convincing, but after we've spent half an hour struggling to get the first pole in place, Helen finally hands the sheet to Ahmid.

"Well?" she demands, as if he should be able to decipher it in ten seconds.

He takes it in his stride. He's been in Arcadia long enough to know how it is. "We need to put up the centre pole first," he says, after a pause. "And we'll need people to hold the four corners. We're going to need more people to help."

"Could we call Freya?" I feel guilty for suggesting it, but we're running out of options. The longer we take doing this, the less time I'll have for the mission.

Helen overhears. "I'll call her now. And some others. We could use extra help with the lights, anyway."

"The lights?" I look at her, surprised.

"Yes, we hang some pretty lights around the marquee and the edges of the field." Helen wanders off to find a call-point. It still surprises me that no one here uses a phone.

I groan and look at Ahmid. "We're never getting out of here are we?"

He pulls a face. "Probably not."

I start to feel more positive when the reinforcements arrive. Freya has an older brother, Jensen, and he seems to have done this before. He's soon getting us organised and shouting orders. I don't care. If he's going to help us finish early, I'll do anything he asks.

With his help, it takes us just over an hour to get the marquee in place.

I wipe sweat from my brow as I stand back and look at it, amazed we managed to erect anything that big.

"Good work, everyone," says Helen, sounding a lot brighter.

"I'm hungry," says Ahmid. "Any chance of a lunch break?"

"I suppose we could take half hour," she allows. "But make sure you come back. There's still a lot of work to do."

"Want to come to mine for something to eat?" asks Freya. "My mum won't mind."

I sigh. "I'd love to, but my uncle's tracking my smart band. I have to stay close to the jetty until at least three."

"Seriously? That's harsh."

As if to underline the point, a few heavy drops of rain land on my head. "And now it's raining. That's just perfect."

"At least you can shelter under the marquee," points out Ahmid. "We'll bring you something back."

"Thanks." I try not to sound like I'm mad at them. It's not their fault I'm stuck here.

They wander off, leaving me alone in the large tent. I peer through the opening across the lake. The sky has turned a lot darker; the rain is going to get worse. It's not a great day to go trekking through the woods to hunt for the stone.

But then I remember the look on my uncle's face after he met with Eugene. The assembly is happening on Monday. If they agree to wipe out the general population, how long will it take to put their plan into action? For all I know, it could happen the next day.

I have to move fast. I can't let a little storm put me off.

I'm the last hope of the Resistance.

And I'm not going to fail.

SEVENTEEN

It takes another hour to string up the lights between the marquee and the surrounding trees.

I wouldn't mind if it wasn't pouring with rain. Even though the active wear is designed for all weathers, Helen has handed out waterproof jackets. That helps keep my top half dry, but my tights are soaking wet and my hair is plastered to my forehead.

"Thanks for inviting me," says Freya, darkly, tying the last of the control boxes in place. "I'd have hated to miss this."

"And you wonder why I hate the outdoors," added Ahmid. "This is why."

"It could be worse," I say. "We could still be camping."

That makes them smile.

I glance at my smart band again. I'm checking it every few minutes, desperate to get away. Only five minutes until I'm free of the eighty-metre boundary around the jetty. Out of the corner of my eye, I see Helen approach.

"Thank you for your help. I think all our guests will be very grateful for the marquee this evening."

We nod and murmur politely. "No problem. You're welcome."

"The good news is that we've finished here. The bad news is that you have to go straight home, Jamie. Your uncle has had reports that you hit someone this morning, so you're grounded."

No, this can't be happening.

"That's a lie."

"You can tell that to your uncle, when he gets home. He wanted me to remind you that he will be monitoring your smart band, so you're not allowed to leave the cabin."

Ahmid cuts in. "Did he say who it was that Jamie hit?"

"A younger boy called Hugh."

I smash my fist into the tree trunk in

frustration. "I'd never do that."

Helen doesn't care. "Like I say, I'm just passing on the message."

As she walks off, I can't help wondering if life is actually easier in lockdown than it is in Arcadia.

"Any idea why Hugh would accuse you of hitting him?" asks Ahmid.

"No. Unless Tyler made him." As soon as I say it, I realise it's true. Tyler has beaten the kid up, and made sure I get the blame. Hugh is probably too scared to tell anyone the truth.

Freya looks concerned. "You don't want to disobey a direct order from your uncle."

"In that case, I better head home."

I kick at the mud as I wander back to the tree house. My plans are in tatters. All I wanted was a few hours to get the metal detector and take it to the stream. It seems that was too much to ask for.

You still need to do this.

I can't let this one setback stop me from completing my mission. Even if I have to disobey my uncle and face the consequences. I wonder whether I should just run off, but I figure that they're tracking my smart band and will be able to trace me. If they catch me before I've had time to search for the copy-token, what will I achieve?

I need a way to hunt in the woods without raising the alarm.

Maybe Ahmid would swap smart bands with me and sit in my room?

No, he's too much of a coward. He's already told me that you'd be stupid to risk anything like that. Taking off your smart band is the closest thing to a criminal offence for a kid in Arcadia.

Who, then?

It doesn't take long to figure it out. There's only one person who might be up for it, who won't be too scared.

The person I hate.

Tyler.

***

I video-call him from my computer as soon as I get in.

"What do you want, turdface?"

I let the insult go. "You're destroying me. I've had enough. You win. I'll do your stupid run."

"Really?" He gives a wicked smile. "The great

Jamie Greaves is finally backing down."

"There's one condition."

He narrows his eyes. "Yeah? What?"

"You have to stay here, in my room, while I do it. If you're wearing my smart band, my uncle will get suspicious if you leave. He grounded me for what I *apparently* did to Hugh."

That makes Tyler chuckle. "I can live with that. I can snooze on your bed while you do 8k in a thunderstorm."

"If I do this, you leave me alone, right?" I say it pathetically, as if he's won.

"Maybe. As long as you *keep* doing it, whenever I need you."

"Every day?"

"If I want."

I groan, as if I'm gutted. But things are coming to a head. I don't think it will be many days before I've completed my mission. "Can you head over here? Right now?"

"Is anyone else in your cabin?"

"No, I'm alone."

He nods. "I'll be there in a few minutes." Then he locks eyes with me. "But just remember, from now on, *I* give the orders."

I hang up and pace around the small room. Outside, lightning flashes across the lake and rain hammers against the window. It's so dark, it feels like dusk. I shudder. It's too late to back out now. If I don't find the copy-token today, who knows how long it will be before I get another chance?

I jump as the door to my room opens. Tyler stands there, drenched from taking the short journey from his cabin to mine. He still has his trainers on as he jumps on my bed, wiping the mud on the duvet just to wind me up. I pretend I don't care.

"Ready to run?" he says. "Nice day for it."

"So, how do we do this?" I ask. "Swap smart bands I mean? Won't they know?"

"Not if we're quick. You just unstrap it and hand it over and I do the same. As long as they're only off for a few seconds, nothing will register."

"Ahmid says you get in a whole heap of trouble if you swap smart bands with someone."

Tyler's lip curls. "Only if they catch you. And trust me, they won't. Not if you don't tell."

"Ok, let's do it."

He reaches for his wrist. "On three. One, two,

three." He removes his smart band in one smooth motion. I fumble for a few seconds with mine, then it comes loose and we swap.

I quickly strap his on my wrist and check the display. There are no warnings; everything looks normal.

"You're good to go." Tyler leans against the wall and looks out the window. "I hope you don't get *too* wet and muddy." He laughs at his own joke.

"You won't leave this room, right?" I'm still worried that he'll give the game away. "My uncle is tracking my band. He's really mad at me right now. If I leave, he'll probably send someone to find me. And then we're both screwed."

"I'll stay right here," says Tyler, "But remember: I want a decent time."

"Sure."

With that, I head off.

I no longer have a waterproof jacket and the rain is coming down with such force, I'm soaked in seconds.

Only one thing makes me smile as I set off toward the supplies cabin. Tyler might think he's won the war, and that he's finally bullied me into submission. But, really, *I'm* using *him*. Now I've got his smart band, rather than my own, I can head off into the woods with the metal detector while he stays in my room. With any luck, my uncle will never know.

But if I stop to search for the fake rock, there's no way I'll complete the run in a decent time. Tyler will probably get punished, but he won't be able to tell anyone what really happened.

Sure, he'll get his own back.

But it'll be worth it.

EIGHTEEN

The rain comes down in sheets. It's like running through a waterfall as I pound through the forest, the metal detector in hand. It's lucky the thing is lightweight, else I'd be cursing a lot more than I already am.

I slosh through deep puddles. I gave up trying to jump them; they're too big and it'll only tire me out. My top and tights are saturated, but they're also trapping the water against my skin and warming up like a wetsuit.

The ground is slippery underfoot, my trainers sliding in the wet mud. My foot catches on a loose root, making me stumble. Water streams off my hair and falls on to my face, sometimes getting in my eyes and making it hard to see. I brush it aside and press on.

The route takes longer than normal.

At least, it seems like it does. The smart band shows my time and distance, and apparently I'm making good progress.

I wonder if Tyler has stayed in my room, like I told him. He's just the sort of kid who doesn't care if he breaks rules like that. It wouldn't surprise me if he left. But I'm hoping that he's too afraid of getting caught swapping smart bands to risk it. Even Tyler seems to recognise the boundaries when it suits him.

I'm also hoping that my uncle doesn't come home early, to get ready for the gathering. That's not likely to happen: he always works late. Still, the sooner I find the copy-token and get back, the less risky it will be.

I force my tired legs to run faster, brushing past wet leaves and jumping fallen logs as I take the barely used path to my destination.

My heart sinks as I burst into the clearing and see the state of the stream. Thankfully, it hasn't burst its banks, but the water is all churned up as the rain lashes down. Trying to find the copy-token was hard enough in the sun. In weather like this, what chance do I stand?

You're crazy, Zac.

Overhead, there's another flash followed by an ominous roll of thunder. Something else to worry about: being hit by lightning.

Now you're just being ridiculous. Get a grip.

I stumble down to the rocks. I've come this far and I'm going to see it through. I resolve to myself that I'm not going back to the settlement until I've found what I'm looking for.

My uncle might discover my deception and ground me for a month. Or the guy who runs the supplies cabin might sign me up for extra community service every weekend. And Tyler already expects me to do his run each day, as well as my own. When I get back, life is going to get increasingly tricky. I'll be lucky if I can find time to sleep, let alone get all the way out here. This could be my last chance.

I hold the metal detector in front of me and switch it on. I check the settings and sweep it over the stones on the bank, hoping that it'll be sensitive enough to detect the copy-token. It's a lot quicker than searching the rocks by hand, that's for sure.

But there's a lot of bank to cover. And there's

also the stream bed. The detector should work underwater; I checked. But that doesn't mean it's going to be fun to traipse up the stream with it in the pouring rain, trying to cover every square inch.

Now I've stopped running, my clothes are starting to cool down. I shiver in the rain as I swing the detector from side to side.

I hope the Resistance appreciate this.

My mates, Kieran and Trix, will be playing pool or making out, oblivious to my suffering here in Arcadia. They've probably forgotten all about me. Everyone else will be in the warm pub, eating Del's home-cooked food and tapping away on computer keyboards. None of them will be cold, wet and miserable.

Still, it's no good feeling sorry for myself. I'm not doing this so people slap me on the back; I'm doing it to try to save millions of lives. I have to remember that, else I'd quit.

Wandering up and down that stream with the metal detector in a thunderstorm is one of the most soul-destroying things I've ever had to do.

The smart band beeps a warning.

No movement detected.

I swear at it, then switch off the detector and jog into the woods. I do a small circuit, just long enough to satisfy the device that I'm not dead, before returning to the stream to resume the search.

That's going to keep happening. Once you're outside a zone, you're expected to keep moving. That means I have to search in spurts, which takes longer.

The rocks are spread out. Some are piled near the stream, others are scattered over the grass where we tried to camp. I can't believe we were only here last night. So much has happened since then.

The detector beeps. There's something metal on the ground. But it's hard to tell what, as it's on the edge of a deep puddle.

I kneel in the mud and plunge my hand into the murky water, hunting around for rocks. There's nothing but mud.

No, wait; there it is again. I can feel something thin and hard. I grab hold and pull it up. It's just a tent peg. I throw it aside and clamber back to my feet, sweeping the ground with the detector, occasionally stopping for another short run. I've already been here forty-five minutes. Tyler's time on this run is going to be so terrible, he'll probably be put on a special diet.

And he'll kill me.

One problem at a time.

Another twenty minutes and there's no sign of the stone. I've had enough. I drop to the ground, exhausted. The rain streams down my face, merging with my tears.

It's no good; I've failed.

"Fat lot of use you are!" I yell at the metal detector. I fling it across the field. It lands on its side, letting out a beep. I've probably damaged it.

That'll earn you another month of community service, Zac.

"So, *now* you want to beep." I wander over, not sure whether I'm gonna try to fix it or kick the thing until it shuts up. I guess I better try to mend it. I might need it again, when I've calmed down.

I notice it's lying next to a stone.

It can't be.

The stone looks the perfect size and shape to be the one I'm after, but I know better than to get my hopes up.

I reach down. It's not as cold as it should be.

And it's not as heavy either. Now, I'm excited. I turn it over, searching for any sign of a secret compartment. My hands shake as I pry at the edge, forcing my nail in to a small opening.

It pops open. And there it is. The copy-token.

I wonder if I'm dreaming. I've been hunting for this thing for so long, I've almost forgotten what it looks like.

I did it!

My tears of frustration turn into a grin of pure joy.

Now, what? I have to get back to the cabin as soon as I can.

My uncle will get home soon, and all hell will break loose if he discovers I'm not in my room and Tyler is there instead.

With the metal detector in one hand and the copy-token in the other, I race back.

NINETEEN

Needless to say, Tyler isn't happy when I finally make it back.

"Over *two and a half hours*."

"I got cramp. Sorry."

He grabs me by the neck and holds me against the wall. "I know what you're up to, Greaves. You thought if you took ages, I wouldn't ask you again."

"I didn't. It wasn't deliberate."

"They'll expect me to run further, thanks to you," he hisses. "And you are going to do every single kilometre."

I can barely breathe, he's choking me so hard. "I will. I promise."

He lets go of my throat and grabs my wrist to remove his smart band. He sees I'm clutching something and prises my fist open. "What's this?"

"Hey, give that back," I say, as he snatches the copy-token. "That's mine."

"Yeah? What is it?"

Now I'm in trouble. I can hardly tell him it's a Resistance hacking device. "It's something my uncle gave me. He told me to take care of it."

Tyler holds it up to the light and examines it closely. "Looks interesting. I might keep it."

"No, please." I reach for the device but he pulls it away.

I've come this far. I can't lose it now.

He can see the desperation on my face, and it feeds his power-complex. "You really want this, don't you?"

I nod. It's too late to pretend it doesn't matter.

"In that case, I'm going to look after it for you. Give me my smart band."

We swap bands. I eye up the copy-token, wondering if I could get it from him in a fight. But there's no way I'd win.

"Please give it back. My uncle might ask me for it. He'll be furious if he thinks I've lost it."

"I'll think about it."

"I'll tell my uncle you stole it."

"Yeah? I doubt it. If you do that, I'll let him know why I was here. I reckon you'd get in more trouble than me. My parents aren't that strict."

With that, Tyler DeBronte leaves, taking the copy-token with him.

I collapse into my chair, wondering how I could be so stupid.

Why didn't I just hide it in my shoe when I took them off at the door? I'd been so tired and desperate to get back, I didn't even think about what would happen if he saw what I was holding.

Now, it's too late.

All my efforts have been for nothing.

I sit there, depressed, watching the rain through the window.

After a while, I decide to get changed. My top and tights will dry, given time, but they're sweaty and filthy and I can't stand the damp feeling any longer. I replace the clothes I'm wearing with identical ones, but at least this set are clean.

The front door slams.

My uncle is home. I head out into the corridor to meet him.

"Jamie, what the hell has been going on?"

I wonder if he knows about my journey into the woods and my deal with Tyler. But then I realise he's talking about something else entirely. "I didn't hit Hugh."

"Really? That's the best you've got?" He glares at me as if he can force the truth out with a look. "Why would he say that you did?"

"Maybe to cover for someone else? Someone he's really afraid of. Like Tyler."

"We're not back to that, are we? Your petty war with the LeBronte kid."

"Fine. Don't believe me. See if I care."

He looks down at me, as if he's working out a complex equation. "We can't carry on like this, Jamie. There's a lot going on right now. It isn't the time to challenge my authority. I've got enough people trying to do that."

"Eugene still giving you grief?"

"And the rest." He sighs and turns, heading into the kitchen.

I follow, uncertain whether he's finished telling me off. "Want me to make you some tea?"

"That would be good." Aaron sits down heavily. "Is this your attempt to suck up to me, so I don't punish you?"

"Something like that." I give a weak smile as I fill up the kettle and switch it on. "Will it work?"

"Maybe. Can't blame you for trying." He looks out the window at the rain. It's starting to ease off. "Not exactly great weather for a gathering."

"I had to put up a marquee this afternoon. We got drenched."

That makes him laugh. "In that case, I guess I had an easier day than you."

You don't know the half of it.

"I don't think Helen knew how to read the instructions," I tell him. "In the end, Freya's brother came to the rescue."

"Jensen? He's a good lad. Natural leader."

We wait for a moment, while the kettle boils. I put a tea-bag in the cup and pour in the water. "You want me to go tonight? Or am I still grounded?"

"You can come. Everyone brings their family."

Family.

The word seems strange, like I no longer know what it means. It's been that long since I've seen my mum and brother, that I've almost forgotten what they look like. And now, here I am, pretending to be this man's nephew and he doesn't even know.

I place the cup in front of him. "Did you never want kids of your own?"

"I was too busy working. Never really had time. Besides, as I'm discovering right now, teenagers are a right pain." He takes a sip of the tea. "This is good."

"Good enough to stop you grounding me for a year?"

"I'll consider it."

"How about if I do you another favour?" I ask.

He can see the mischievous glint in my eye, and it piques his curiosity. "What did you have in mind?"

"I could punch Eugene in the face. He'd never know you asked me to."

He actually laughs at that, so hard that tea spurts out of his nose. "That's kind of tempting. Let me think on it."

"Sure. I'd be happy to help."

TWENTY

"Looks like the rain finally stopped," says Aaron, as we stroll towards the jetty.

"Great," I say, drily. "That makes me feel so much better about all those hours I spent putting up the marquee."

He slaps me on the back as if we're old mates. "Cheer up. Tonight should be fun."

"I hope so."

I could sure use some fun. It seems like such a long time since I had any. I can barely remember what it's like.

The clearing is heaving with people, wandering in and out of the marquee, drinks in hand. Now it's all lit up, the place looks amazing. Maybe all the effort *was* worth it. I can hear a band playing jazz.

Aaron nudges me. "Looks like your favourite person volunteered to help tonight."

"What?"

"Over to the left, by the entrance."

I'm surprised to see Tyler holding a tray of drinks, offering them to people who walk past. "No way did he volunteer."

"Maybe he's not as bad as you think?"

I've only just got on good terms with my uncle. I'm not about to risk another disagreement. "Maybe."

My uncle takes a drink from another silver tray as we enter. I reach for one, but he slaps my hand. "These are for the grown-ups. There will be some kind of non-alcoholic punch for you. Look, on that table, over there." He points to the far corner.

"Mind if I get some?"

"Feel free."

I wander over, weaving in and out among the adults. Some of the faces are familiar. You can't live in a community as close-knit as the red zone without getting to know a lot of people. But there are others I've never seen before. Presumably, some of them work in the Nexus.

I reach the table and ladle some of the drink from the large bowl into a glass. The punch is red, sweet and fizzy. Not that I'm complaining. Most of the time, I only get to drink water.

"Your uncle let you out, then?" I turn to see Ahmid standing behind me, holding a plate of food.

"Yeah, in the end. He's not as strict as you think. Not when you get to know him."

Ahmid bites into something and makes a face of pure delight. "You have to try one of these spring rolls."

"Where did you get them?"

"I'll show you." He leads me through the crowd.

"Hey, did you see Tyler handing out drinks? What's with that? Is that some kind of community service?"

"No, he always volunteers."

I grab Ahmid's shoulder. "Are we talking about the same kid?"

He nods. "He knows it's the only way to get his hands on some alcohol. At the start of the night, he's as good as gold, handing out drinks. At the end, he slips away with a few mates and they have their own little party."

"Figures." I knew he'd have an ulterior motive.

We reach the buffet table. I pick up a clean plate from the pile while Ahmid piles on even more stuff. I'm impressed by the selection of food. Since I arrived in Arcadia, I've been surprised at how varied a vegan diet can be. But tonight, they've really gone to town.

"Freya's here, down by the lake. And a few others."

I hesitate and scan the crowd. "I'm not sure if I'm allowed to join you. I better check with my uncle. I told him I was getting a drink."

"I guess you're on thin ice."

"You have no idea. If I do anything else wrong, he'll probably have me thrown out of this place." I'm only half joking.

Ahmid shakes his head. "No one leaves Arcadia. You can't. It's a rule."

"Good to know." It does make me wonder what happens to bad people instead. But now is not the time to ask. "I better get back."

I leave him by the buffet table, wondering if there will be any food left for everyone else by the time he's finished.

It takes me a while to locate my uncle, but he appears to be in a deep conversation with a woman. I hover nearby, not sure whether to interrupt. From their expressions, it's clear this isn't a romantic encounter. I can just about make out what they're saying over the background noise.

"Is there any chance we'll lose the vote?" he says.

"Hard to say. The senate seem split down the middle."

"It's insane they'd even consider it. I'll never allow it." He glances around and sees me lurking. "Ah, Jamie. There you are. You found the food table, I see. Janine, this is my nephew."

"You must be the new arrival." Janine tries to smile, but seems too worried to pull it off. "How long have you been here now?"

"Two weeks, but it feels longer."

"For both of us," adds Aaron, attempting a joke.

Now I'm here, they don't seem to know what to say to one another. There's an awkward silence.

I rescue them. "Ahmid and Freya are down by

the lake. They asked me to join them."

Aaron looks relieved. "I'm sure that would be more fun than hanging around in here with an old fossil like me."

I wonder if I've offended him. "I can stay here if you prefer?"

"It's fine. You go and play."

He says it like I'm five, but I don't care, as long as I can get away.

I slip off into the crowd, heading for the exit.

Tyler intercepts, still holding the tray of drinks. "Where are you off to?" he asks.

"Just down to the lake."

He steps forward, getting right in my face. I can smell alcohol on his breath. "Ok, but don't go home. We need you later."

"Yeah?"

"We're having a little gathering of our own. Me and the boys."

I try to act casual. "Good for you. But if it's all the same, I'll give it a miss."

"No, you won't. Not if you want your little trinket back." He smirks at me, knowing I can't refuse.

"Fine, I'll come."

"You better."

Curiosity gets the better of me. "Why would you even want me there?"

A wicked grin spreads across his face. "Because you're the entertainment."

TWENTY-ONE

Two hours later, I'm summoned by Tyler.

He's hanging out in the almost-empty storage shed with two of his mates, Kyle and Jack. They've set out a few old chairs and a folding table, which is covered with empty glasses and half-full bottles. The place is lit by candles. It reeks of booze and they look like they've already had too much.

"Here he is, the nephew of our great founder."

I'm not gonna lie; I'm pretty scared. Tyler is bad news at the best of times. Who knows what he's capable of when he's drunk. I stand in front of them, feeling awkward.

"What do you want, Tyler?"

"It's what *you* want that matters, Jamie." He holds up the copy-token. It glints in the candlelight. I wonder if he's so far gone that I can just grab it and run, but I don't think it would end well. With his friends here, I'd never make it out of the door.

"What's that?" asks Jack, interested.

"Something his uncle gave him," smirks Tyler. "Something really valuable, apparently. Be a shame if it ended up in the lake."

"My uncle will kill you if you do that." I try to sound like it will be his problem, not mine.

"Yeah? I reckon if that were true, you'd have already told him I took it from you. I don't think he even knows you have this. You probably stole it from him."

I gulp. "That's not true."

Tyler gives a wicked grin. "Either way, let's find out how badly you want it back. What should we make Jamie do, lads?"

"Make him dance," suggests Kyle.

"Yeah, naked," adds Jack, with a grin.

Please, no.

Thankfully, Tyler speaks up. "I don't want to see that. I might have nightmares."

That makes them laugh.

"We're not being very hospitable," points out

Jack. "We could at least give him a drink."

"Yeah, it's only polite." Kyle picks a half-empty bottle off the table. He walks over to me and holds it out.

"I'm fine, thanks."

Tyler raises his eyebrows. "Drink it, Jamie."

"If I do, will I get my property back?"

"It's a start."

I take the bottle and try not to think about what's inside. I hold it to my lips and knock it back. The liquid tastes like cat-pee and burns my throat. I break out coughing.

"Little Jamie never had a drink before." Jack says it in a high-pitched voice like he's talking to a baby.

"You have to finish it," adds Kyle. "You barely took a sip."

I lift the bottle and gulp down the sour contents. As soon as I've finished, I feel like I want to throw up.

Tyler finishes his own drink and wipes his mouth with his arm. "Now, you can dance."

"I-I-I don't know how."

"Quit whining and dance!" Jack gives me a hard kick to the backside.

I shuffle awkwardly from side to side, feeling ridiculous.

The lads are in hysterics.

"How about some ballet?" suggests Kyle.

"Yeah, let's see a pirouette," adds Jack.

"A what?" I have no idea what he's talking about.

"Hands in the air, then twirl around on your tiptoes."

I groan. "Seriously?"

They urge me on like baying hyenas. I straighten up and do my best to give them what they want, but lose my balance and almost crash into the table. That just makes them laugh even more.

I climb to my feet, my face burning. "You've had your fun. Give me the device."

"First, you have to kneel down and lick the bottom of my shoes." Tyler leans back in his chair and holds up his foot.

"You can't be serious."

"I think he needs another drink first," suggests Jack, but instead of handing me a bottle, he pours one over me. It streams over my hair and face.

I wipe the worst off with the back of my hand, trying to act like I don't care. But my self-esteem has hit rock bottom. I've been through some tough stuff, being a member of the Resistance, but this is a new low.

"Well?" Tyler looks at me, expectantly. He really expects me to do this.

I drop to my knees and stick out my tongue. I let it touch the sole of his trainer then pull back.

"That doesn't count," shouts Jack. "You have to actually lick it properly."

"Right from the back to the front," agrees Kyle.

"Get on with it," demands Tyler.

I've come this far. I guess I don't have any dignity left to lose. I lick the shoe. It tastes of dirt and grit. At least this time, they seem satisfied.

"This is *too* funny," says Jack. "Best night ever."

"Have you finished?" I ask, hoping they're all out of ideas.

No such luck.

Tyler looks thoughtful. "There must be something else we can make him do. Something epic."

"We could make him swim the lake?" suggests

Kyle. "It'll be freezing tonight."

"Nah, it's too public. People will see."

There's a moment of quiet while they contemplate my fate.

"I have an idea," mutters Jack.

Tyler looks interested. "Yeah? What?"

Jack wanders over and whispers something in his ear.

"That *is* epic."

My stomach turns. "What?"

"We're not telling you. Not yet. But you need to come with us."

TWENTY-TWO

They lead me through the red zone.

A few people are out and about, but they have no idea of the trouble I'm in. All they see are four lads, laughing and joking. Well, the others are doing that. I just walk alongside them, wondering what they're planning.

I'm tempted to run. But if I do, I'll never get the copy-token back. Besides, they'd probably catch me, and things would get worse. I have to see this through, however humiliating it is.

"This is gonna be so funny," says Jack, glancing in my direction.

That doesn't make me feel any better.

Initially, I assume they're taking me to one of the communal buildings like the sports centre, but we take the path that leads to the tennis courts, away from the main settlement and into the more deserted part of the forest.

Here, the only light comes from a device that Kyle is holding. The trees cast large shadows and my fear grows. I can't even call for help. No one will hear me. Whatever these boys are intending to do, it's going to be bad.

"Are we nearly there?" I ask.

"Not far," smirks Tyler. "Not feeling so cocky now, are we?"

"I've done everything you asked. I just want my token back."

"And you'll get it. Very soon."

That's good news, if he's being serious.

What isn't so reassuring is we branch off towards the compost shed. We step into a small clearing and the corrugated steel structure looms in front of us.

"Been here before, Jamie?" asks Jack.

"Of course, he has," says Kyle. "He lives here."

That brings on another round of laughter, all at my expense.

"In we go," says Tyler. He grabs hold of my shoulder and pushes me towards the door. He probably thinks I might try to run, now I know where we're heading. He's not wrong.

"Wh-What are you going to do?" I can't hide the fear from my voice. As the door swings open, the overpowering smell floods my nostrils, making me gag. The light flickers on, stupidly bright after being outside in the dark woods.

We're standing on the small wooden platform. Only a low railing separates us from the stinking pit below, full of rotten vegetables, worms and beetles.

"It's time to see just how badly you want this," says Tyler, holding up the copy-token. "Enough to jump in the pit?"

I shake my head. "I won't do it."

"You sure?" He pulls back his arm and throws the device to the far end, where it plops into the compost.

Noooooooooooooo.

I want to scream and shout at him, but it's no good. It'll only make them laugh. Instead, I fix my eyes on where the token landed. I need to remember that spot. With any luck, it hasn't gone too deep.

"Well? Are you gonna fetch it or what?" Jack folds his arms, blocking the exit.

I stand my ground. "I'm not jumping in that. I'm not that desperate."

Not with you lot watching, anyway.

Once they've gone, I'm going to have to try to retrieve the device. Even though the pit is the most disgusting thing I've ever seen, I can't let the Resistance down.

"Shame. We'll have to do this the hard way." Jack steps towards me. "Come on, lads."

I feel hands grabbing hold of me, hauling me off my feet. Tyler has me by the arms and the two others have one of each of my legs.

"No, don't," I cry, as they start to swing me from side to side.

But to them, this is all a game.

"On three," says Tyler. He counts up with each swing. "One... Two... Three..."

With that, they let go, throwing me over the railing and into the pit.

I land on my front with a squelch. Something splashes into my mouth as I push my body upright. But it's like sinking sand or soft mud. If I try to stand, I sink down to my waist. I'm covered in filth. As I look down, I see slugs on my chest. Something is crawling in my sodden hair and I frantically brush it with my hands.

Tyler, Jack and Kyle are laughing. Seeing me in the pit is the highlight of their night.

"Sure you don't want your device back?" says Tyler. "It's only over the other side."

"Screw you." I manoeuvre myself over to the railing. I reach up to pull myself out.

Jack screws up his nose. "Ew, he stinks."

"Even worse than usual," says Kyle. That makes them laugh some more.

"Come on, let's get out of here," says Jack. "Someone might come."

The three boys turn to leave, but Tyler looks at me, clinging to the railing, dripping with filth. "Next time you do my run, make sure you get a decent time. Or this happens again."

He doesn't wait for a response, just leaves. I can hear their voices as they head away from the compost shed and back into the woods.

I drag myself on to the platform. I want to follow them, to get out of this place with its pungent smell and creepy-crawlies. But somewhere at the other side of this pit is the copy-token. I know I can't leave it. If I'd got it back with the boys watching, I was worried they'd take it from me again. Now that they've gone, that's no longer an issue. They think I've given up on it. Any sane person would.

I glance over at the far side. I've memorised where the thing landed. But who knows how far it sank? The pit is a mix of solid and liquid, squelchy compost and fetid water. If I'm not careful, even moving towards it might send it deeper.

But what else can I do?

I take a deep breath and use the platform to jump as far across the pit as I can. This time, I land upright, the compost reaching above my waist. I'm so deep, I can barely move. I wonder if it would be possible to drown in this stuff. It's not a pleasant thought.

Get on with it, Zac.

I'm half-walking, half-swimming across the pit. Worms cling to my arms as I push myself forward. Something crawls up my neck. As fast as I try to get rid of the creepy-crawlies, more appear, keen to explore my body.

My best bet is to move fast and try to ignore them. I slosh over to the right spot, then hunt around with my hands, hoping I'll feel the cold, shiny metal in the midst of the muck. But here, the sludge is thin and watery. The token will have sunk right down.

I've come this far.

I plunge under the surface, my whole head immersed in the filth. I push myself as deep as I can, my hands searching for the device. I can feel stringy vegetables and mouldy fruit. This makes hunting for the fake rock look easy. I can't hold my breath much longer.

I break the surface, gasping for air. By now, I'm used to the smell. That can't be a good thing. As soon as I've got my breath back, I plunge down again, wondering how long I can keep this up. If Tyler and his friends had hung around, they'd have one hell of a show, watching me dive into the gunk.

I lose track of time, wallowing in the filth and in my own dark misery.

But it's worth it.

I feel a coin. I grasp for it, but then it's gone. It can't be far. I'm sure it was the copy-token. I move much more carefully now, not wanting to lose the location. Before long, I sense it again. This time, I grab hold and bring it to the surface.

I have it!

As I hold it up, dripping with brown muck, I wonder if it will still work. The Resistance told me it was waterproof. I can only hope that's true.

I force my body back, wading through the muck, then climb out the pit. One by one, I remove the slugs and worms from my body and brush off the beetles, then head out the door into the darkness.

I can't head home like this. It will raise way too many questions. First, I have to get clean. And there's only one way to do that without going back to my cabin.

I head to the lake.

TWENTY-THREE

The water is freezing.

My teeth chatter as I wade further out. The lake is calm at this time of night. I'm some way from the gathering, having chosen a spot much further along the shore.

I force my head under, massaging my hair with my hands, keen to wash out any remaining muck. This water isn't exactly clean, but it'll do. Anything has to be better than the filth of the compost pit.

By the time I emerge, dripping and shivering, I've washed off the brown sludge. I'm hoping my uncle has already headed home and gone to bed. But the chances are, he's still up, having a late-night drink. And that means I have to be able to explain why I'm so wet.

Sure enough, the lights are still on as I squelch up the ramp to our tree house. I slip the copy-token down the front of my tights for safe-keeping. As I open the door, Aaron meets me in the hallway.

He's shocked to see the state I'm in. "What happened to you?"

"Me and some mates. We were in the mood for a boat ride. I lost my footing when we climbed out."

"There always has to be some drama, doesn't there? You couldn't just eat and chat to people like everyone else."

"Sorry." I feel like I keep letting him down.

He shakes his head and returns to the kitchen. I follow him some of the way, hovering in the doorway.

"Did you have a good night?" I ask, trying to ease the tension.

"Not really." He looks up at me with sad eyes. "I'm going to have to work tomorrow. There's a lot to do before the big meeting on Monday evening."

"The assembly?"

He nods. "Without some kind of

breakthrough, they're going to vote against me, I know it."

"You'll figure something out."

"I hope so." A brief pause. "Do you have any plans tomorrow?"

Tread carefully, Zac.

"I promised Ahmid I'd help with his robot, after letting him down today."

"I wondered if you'd like to come and see the Nexus first? I'd like to show you around."

It seems a strange offer when he's so busy. I wouldn't have thought he'd have time to give me a tour. But I'm not complaining. I need to get inside that place.

"That would be awesome."

"You'll need to be ready by eight."

"I can do that." I'm still shivering as I stand there. "But right now, I need a hot shower."

"Go." He makes a gesture with his hand, like he's swatting a fly.

Relieved, I head to my room.

Whatever is about to happen here in Arcadia really has him riled up. Aaron Greaves is worried.

And I wonder if I should be too.

***

I'm dressed and ready for 7.45am. I don't want to risk missing out on my opportunity to get inside the Nexus. This is the best chance I have to plant the copy-token.

"You look keen," comments Aaron, sipping his coffee.

"I am."

"Then let's go."

I was hoping there might be time for breakfast, but I follow him out. We wander down the wooden walkway. I can see a blue sky through the canopy of trees, but the undergrowth is still wet. Everything smells fresh.

"Does every zone have a Nexus?" I ask, partly out of interest and partly to make conversation.

"No. Just the red zone. Our focus is on computers and communications with the outside world."

In other words: hacking.

"What do the others focus on?"

"The yellow zone is all about biology and medicine. They deal with the vaccine and keeping everyone healthy. The green zone develops the technology to prevent climate change."

"What about blue?"

"They're meant to be dealing with politics and policies, finding ways to help society navigate the tremendous changes we need to face. Not that they're doing a great job of it."

"I thought Ahmid said there were five zones?"

"Sort of," he allows. "The white zone is a bit different. It handles supplies here in Arcadia. That's where we grow all the food and where the clothing is produced."

It doesn't take long to reach the Nexus. The building is shaped like a massive octagon, rising three stories into the air, all glass and polished wood. There appears to only be one entrance, and we head towards it. I'm interested to see what the security is like.

"There shouldn't be anyone else here today," says Aaron. "We try to make sure everyone has Sundays off."

The way he says it makes me wonder if he's breaking the rules, bringing me here. "Am I not meant to go inside?"

"Not really," he admits. "But there have to be

some advantages to being in charge, right?" He gives me a reassuring smile.

The door opens as we approach. "Isn't there a key code or something? Can anyone walk in?"

"The Nexus knows it's me," he says, mysteriously.

"How?" I need to work this out, or I have no hope of breaking in. Even if I plant the copy-token today, I'll need to come back to collect it once it's harvested the data.

Aaron holds up his wrist. "Because of this."

The smart band. Of course. That's how they keep track of everyone. It makes sense that whenever authorised people approach, the Nexus knows it's them.

Inside, there are smooth desks, laid out in concentric circles, a bit like in school. But in this place, everyone faces outwards, towards the windows. Each desk has a seat, a screen and a keyboard. At the centre of the room, a spiral staircase leads to the upper floors.

As Aaron expected, the place is deserted.

"This way," he says, leading me to the staircase. "I work upstairs."

The second floor is almost identical to the

first, an open plan area laid out with desks. But the top floor is different. Here there are actual rooms. Four doors lead off the landing.

He opens one and walks through. "This is my office."

It's impressive. There's a large desk which curves down to merge with the floor at one end. The walls around the edge are solid glass, with sliding doors leading out to a large balcony. At this end of the room, comfortable seats form a small meeting area. Bookcases line the other walls; a kaleidoscope of colour in the otherwise neutral space.

"That's a lot of books," I say, unable to hide my surprise. I haven't seen any in Arcadia.

He gives me a conspiratorial smile. "My guilty pleasure. In the future, everything will be digital. But these already exist, and it seems a shame to throw them away."

I wander over to the window and look out. "I can see what you spend so much time here."

He laughs. "Trust me. It's not for the view. I have a lot to do. And this is where it happens." He settles at the desk and brings the computer to life. "Right, are you watching carefully, Zac? I'm about to type in my password."

For a moment, I think I've misheard. The idea that he's willing to show me his password seems unbelievable, ridiculous. Why would he do that?

But then I realise that's not even the strangest thing.

There was something else very wrong with what he just said.

Something that changes the game entirely.

He called me Zac.

TWENTY-FOUR

I stare at him, my mouth open.

There doesn't seem to be any point denying who I am.

"You know."

"Of course."

I suddenly feel hot, like it's a hundred degrees. I tug at my collar, wishing the top wasn't so tight. "But, that..."

I trail off. My brain is doing somersaults, trying to keep up. Nothing makes sense.

"Have a seat." Aaron leads me over to the couch. He sits opposite, his foot resting on his knee. It's clear who's in charge. "Perhaps I should fill you in?"

I can't find any words, so settle for a non-committal noise. "Uh, huh?"

"We've been aware of the Resistance for some time. They caused no end of disruption. When they got hold of the plans for Arcadia, we were worried. We had to stop them. The problem was, they were hard to find."

I could understand that. No one would have suspected the derelict pub in my old town as a Resistance hideout.

Aaron's lip curls. "So, we laid out some bait."

Realisation dawns on me. "Jamie. The whole thing was a set-up?"

"That's right. I don't actually have a nephew. But we made up a back-story and planted one of our best teenage hackers in a house in London, and had him send a desperate message to me, as if I was his uncle. We made sure the Resistance had every chance to intercept it, and they didn't disappoint."

I know what happened next. "They kidnapped him."

"That's right. Just as we hoped. The whole point was to get him inside the Resistance operation so he could find a way to contact us with the location."

"But they locked him up so he couldn't go near

any computers."

Aaron shrugs. "We guessed they might. But he's a cute kid. We figured he'd talk his way out of being a prisoner. He's only twelve, and I get the impression the Resistance aren't as hard-hearted as they make out."

I feel sick. When Jamie had first been taken to our Resistance base, he'd been chained in the toilets. It was me who convinced them to let him out. "So where do I come into this?"

"You were a pleasant surprise," he admits. "We guessed they'd kidnap Jamie. We didn't know they'd try to replace him."

"But what use am I to you?" I wonder if the door is locked, or whether I can make a run for it. But, even if I escape the Nexus, I'm still stuck in Arcadia.

"You know where the Resistance are," he points out.

"I'd never tell."

"Let's be clear about something, Zac. If I wanted information out of that little head of yours, I have ways of making you talk." He says it in such a matter-of-fact way, it makes my blood run cold. The thing is, he's probably right. I'd never cope with being tortured. "As things stand, Jamie has already sent us everything we need to locate one of the hideouts. That should lead us to the others."

That's not good. I have to warn them.

But I still have loads of unanswered questions. "So, why keep pretending I'm your nephew? Why not lock me up the moment I arrive?"

Aaron stands up and wanders over to the window. "I could have. Instead, I let you live with me where I could keep a close eye on you. I made sure you were too busy to get up to too much mischief. I wanted you to experience life here, to understand why this place was built. We're saving the world, Zac. Surely, you can see that?"

"You're worried about climate change. I get it."

"More than worried. The world is dying. Arcadia is our last hope."

"Does everyone else know? That I'm not really your nephew?"

"It's our little secret. Only a few people know the truth. Most people wouldn't appreciate me inviting a Resistance spy into our compound."

"No kidding."

"And there's something else." He looks over at me. There's a strange look in his eyes. Is that desperation? "I might need your help."

Of all the revelations, this is the most surprising. I lean forward, not sure if I heard correctly. "Why?"

"There's an assembly tomorrow. There's going to be a vote. The Senate are restless. They want to release the vaccine."

"They should." I say it stubbornly, like I'm still his rebellious nephew. "I know what you told me before, about waiting until you can prevent climate change. But if you have a vaccine, you should share it with the world."

"The real vaccine, maybe."

It takes a moment for the penny to drop. "There's a fake one?"

"They call it Plan B." He sits back down, his restless energy making me nervous. "I should never have allowed it. I didn't know it would come to this."

I think of my mum and my brother, out there in the real world. "What exactly does this fake vaccine do?"

"Possibly nothing," replies Aaron. "It may just

be a placebo."

I relax. "That doesn't sound so bad."

"No? Imagine what it will be like. Everyone comes out of lockdown and life returns to normal. They think they're immune to Vicron-X. Before anyone realises, it's too late. The virus has spread like wildfire through the population. Almost half of them die."

I gulp. "I didn't think of that."

He rubs his face. "But that's only the weakest version of Plan B. It might be worse. They might use the apocalypse strain."

"The apocalypse strain?" My throat feels so tight, I can barely say the words.

"It's a new virus. Worse than Vicron-X. At first, everyone will seem fine. They'll go about their lives as if nothing has happened. About three weeks later, they'll start to drop dead. By then, everyone will be infected. It will be too late to stop it. The entire population will be wiped out."

"Except for the people living here, in Arcadia?"

He nods. "When you get the brightest minds in the country to work on a difficult problem, they sometimes come up with undesirable solutions."

"I can't believe that the people here would ever do that. They seem so nice."

"Most people here don't know about Plan B. They just think we're debating the best timing for the proper vaccine rollout."

I clench my fists. "We have to stop them."

"We're going to." Aaron beckons me over to the computer. "The reason I haven't wiped out the Resistance base is because I knew we might need outside help if Plan B was ever put into action."

"That's smart."

He looks at me, bemused that he's being complimented by a teenager. "Thanks. But if the Resistance are going to join us, we need to persuade them that the vaccine is poisoned."

"Can't you just message them? I mean, you got them to intercept Jamie's message."

"They'll never believe anything that comes from me. They need to hear it from you."

"I'll send them a message. Tell them what's happening. They're expecting me to hack your network so they'll be expecting me to contact them."

He lets out a derisive snort. "Then they're stupider than I thought. Without me, you wouldn't stand a chance of accessing the network."

"Maybe." Aaron has no idea I have the copy-token, but even with it, breaking in to the network would be difficult. It'll be much easier if he just gives me his password. I wonder if wading through the compost was a waste of time. "Why are you showing me now? Why not wait for the vote?"

"I get the feeling that by then, it may be too late." He doesn't elaborate. Instead, he gestures to the keyboard. "Watch closely."

I memorise the string of letters, numbers and symbols that form his password. Once we're in, he shows me how to navigate the unusual operating system.

"You start by typing…"

We both hear a noise. Footsteps on the spiral staircase. More than one person is coming in this direction.

"Quick. Hide." Aaron points to the seating area.

I dive behind the sofa. Seconds later, the door swings open.

"Ah, Aaron, I thought I might find you here." It's Eugene. I can tell by the voice. "Working on a Sunday?"

"Just catching up. You know how it is."

"I'm afraid we can't let you do that. I'm worried that you're about to leak confidential information. These men are here to arrest you."

"Are you out of your mind?" demands Aaron. "I've done nothing wrong. And I'm the leader of the Senate."

"Not any more."

"You can't vote me out. Not until the assembly are gathered."

"We changed the rules, Aaron. You and your allies have been removed from office. Arcadia is under new leadership. You will be kept in a secure location where you can't interfere as we roll out Plan B."

"This is an outrage. What do you think you're doing?"

Eugene's answer is as unexpected as it is cold. "Saving humanity."

With that, they drag Aaron away, his protests

falling on deaf ears.

That leaves me alone, here in the Nexus, crouching behind a sofa.

The only person in the Resistance who knows what's about to happen.

The last hope of the free world.

TWENTY-FIVE

The room seems different without Aaron. As I take my place at the grand desk, I glance out the window, feeling exposed. It doesn't matter. This shouldn't take long. All I have to do is log in using his password and get a message to the Resistance. After that, with any luck, I can patch them in so they can hack the network and defeat the Collective.

I type the password. The screen changes to show the command-line interface. Aaron hadn't finished showing me how to use it, but I can figure it out. I've been trained by the best hackers in the Resistance. How hard can it be?

I execute a web browser and hunt for one of the online chat rooms which the Resistance use for their coded communications. Now, all I have to do is send a message. I start typing it out, a stark warning about the vaccine being poisoned, and the details they'll need to hack into the Nexus from outside. I use a cipher of course. I don't want the Collective to intercept the message.

I'm just about to send it when everything shuts down. The screen goes blank, like there's been a power cut. I wait a few seconds, wondering if it will come back on, but then I realise it's too much of a coincidence for a random outage. I head out the door and creep down the stairs, wondering if someone knows I'm here. If they do, I'm screwed. There's only one way out and they'll have that covered.

I can hear voices on the ground floor.

"That's the power off." The man says it like he's fixed the toilet.

"To the whole Nexus? Are you sure?"

"Yeah. They won't be able to turn it back on. Not without this core."

"Good. Give that to Eugene."

"Come on, let's go."

"How do we get out? The door's stuck."

"I'll sort it." The technician fiddles with the

box next to it, disconnecting the magnetic lock.

Then, they leave, taking a piece of the Nexus with them. I'm relieved that they don't know I'm here, but by shutting down the network they've stopped me from contacting the Resistance. Now, there's no way I can get them a message. The Collective will release one of their fake vaccines, and millions of people will die.

I can't let that happen.

Think, Zac.

I have to get out of here.

I may not be able to send a message over the net, but I can still tell the Resistance in person. They'll listen to me, I know they will. But that means I need to escape from Arcadia.

I creep down the stairs and sneak across to the door. Once I'm outside, I head for the communal stores.

I have no idea what to do or who I can trust.

But I know where the fence is, the one that surrounds Arcadia.

And if I can get myself some bolt cutters, I might escape.

***

I'm only halfway there when I realise the huge flaw in my plan.

The smart band will track me the entire way. If I escape, it'll probably trigger some kind of alarm. But if I take it off, it will also register that something is wrong. I have to get rid of it.

There are two people I could ask: Ahmid or Freya.

Ahmid's a nice guy, but he's also a coward. He'd never have the guts to help me out. Not in the way I need.

So, Freya it is.

I jog through the red zone. Hardly anyone is about. I guess they were up late at the gathering. Once I'm standing beneath the tree house where Freya lives with her family, I look up, wondering how to get her attention. Maybe I should have gone back to my place and called her through the computer instead?

It's too late for that now. I know which room she sleeps in, so I pick up a small stone and hurl it at the window. It bounces off, hardly making any noise. I try a bigger stone, wondering if she's a really heavy sleeper.

"Oi, lad. If you break my window, there'll be trouble." I turn around to see Freya's dad walking towards me, a bag of supplies in his hand.

I step back, flustered. "Sorry. I just want to speak to Freya."

"You could always knock, like a civilised person."

I feel the blood rushing to my cheeks. "Yeah, sorry."

"Come on. I'll tell her you're here." He leads me up the ramp and along a hanging walkway to the front door. As soon as it's open, he yells for her. "Freya, your boyfriend's here."

I'm not sure whether to tell him we're not dating, but I'm guessing he knows that. It's probably just his little joke.

"You want something to drink?" he asks, leading me through to the kitchen.

"No. I'm good, thanks." I stand around awkwardly until Freya appears, looking confused.

"Jamie, what gives?"

"Sorry to call so early. I, err, I need some help with the essay." It's a feeble excuse, but she takes the hint.

"I can talk you through it. Why don't you come to my room."

"Leave the door open," warns her dad. "I'm sure Jamie is a nice boy, but you know the rules."

"Don't worry. I will."

Freya's room is almost identical to mine. She pulls me in, leaving the door ajar. "I'm guessing you're not here about homework?"

"What gives it away?"

"The fact that you never do that until the night before." Freya sits on the bed and looks up at me. "So, why *are* you here?"

"I need your help." I glance behind me, worried that someone will overhear.

"It's ok, Dad's still in the kitchen."

"Some men arrested my uncle this morning."

"No way." Freya sits up a little straighter. "What for?"

"There's a big fall out about the vote that's taking place on Monday. But there's something he asked me to do. I have to take a message to someone outside Arcadia." I decide not to tell her it's for the Resistance. She doesn't need to know all the details.

"On the outside? But, you can't leave. No one can."

"I'm going to use some bolt cutters on the fence."

"Bolt cutters?"

"I figure there might be some in the communal store."

Freya stands up and grabs me by the shoulders. "What you're planning is suicide. You can't just break out. Beyond the first fence are motion detectors with lasers. Anything that moves gets shot. Even if by some miracle you get past those, there's another fence at the outer boundary, one that's made of solid steel bars. Bolt cutters won't make a dent. The only way through the fence is via the main gates which are guarded twenty-four seven."

I pull away from her grasp and look out the window. "How do you know?"

"We learnt about it in class, when we first arrived, in case we tried to leave for a dare or something."

"They really don't want us to escape, do they?" My plan seems stupid now. I feel like a little kid who's been caught trying to run away.

"To be fair, I think they're more worried about anyone else getting in." Freya frowns, deep in thought. "Why did you think I could help?"

"I need someone to take my smart band, so they don't realise where I'm going."

"That's a big ask, Jamie."

"I know."

There's an awkward silence.

"There must be some other way out," I say, eventually, wishing it were true. "My uncle would know. He knew everything about this place. But now he's gone."

Freya glances at me as if she's going to say something, then changes her mind and looks away.

"What? What is it?"

"It's just..." She brushes her hair out of her eyes. She can see I'm not going to let up until she tells me. "Your uncle wasn't the only founder of Arcadia."

This hardly seems the time for a history lesson, so why is she telling me?

Unless...

"You mean, someone else might know another way out?"

She nods. "If there is one, the other founders would know about it."

"Who are they?"

"There are two others. One is called Eugene, and he lives near here. He's your best bet."

My heart sinks. "He's the guy who arrested my uncle. I can't ask him."

"Oh."

"Who's the other?"

"I don't think he'll be any use."

I wonder if she's trying to drive me mad. "Just tell me, Freya. It's important."

"We call him Old Man Devlin."

"So why can't I ask him?"

"Because he'll shoot you."

TWENTY-SIX

It takes me a moment to process what Freya said.

"You can't be serious?" I ask her.

"He went a bit crazy. Cut himself off from the rest of us."

"But he's here? In Arcadia?"

"He lives like a hermit in the forest, somewhere outside the green zone. But he doesn't like visitors. We've all been warned to stay away."

"Some paradise this turned out to be," I mutter. "How do I find him?"

"I don't think you're hearing me. He's dangerous. Someone tried to talk to him once and ended up with a bullet in their leg. I'm not exaggerating. The man's lost it. He's paranoid and violent."

I stare at her, defiant. "But he might know a way out."

"It's not worth the risk. Just face the facts: you can't escape."

"Freya, if I don't get this message to the outside, millions of people could die."

Her eyes go wide. "What? How?"

"They're planning to release a fake vaccine. One that will kill people."

"They'd never do that."

"They call it Plan B."

She swears, softly, under her breath.

I press on. "Eugene and his buddies think it's the only way to save the planet. My uncle didn't agree. That's why they arrested him."

She swears again, louder this time.

I glance at the open door, worried that her dad will hear. "Will you help me or not?"

She rolls her eyes. "Yes, Jamie, if it's that important, I'll help you. But don't blame me if you get yourself killed."

***

We walk to the edge of the red zone.

"You sure you'll be able to find it?" she asks.

"I will now," I say, holding up a map she gave me. Thanks to her, I've worked out the quickest route to Old Man Devlin's place.

"I'd come with you, if I could."

"That would kind of defeat the purpose of you having my smart band. I really appreciate you doing this."

She looks at her wrists and smiles. "How long do you think it will take them to realise I'm wearing two?"

"Maybe hold your arms apart every now and again, just to keep them fooled."

Without warning, she leans forward and kisses me hard on the lips. I'm so shocked I almost fall back.

"Good luck, Jamie."

I wonder whether I should tell her my real name is Zac.

I decide against it. That will just spoil the moment and raise a lot of questions I'd rather not answer.

"Thanks. You too."

As I walk away, she calls after me: "If you die, I'll kill you."

That makes me smile. "I'll keep that in mind."

I push my way past some bushes, and further into the woods.

I haven't gone far before I hear a scream. It's Freya.

"Get off! Leave me alone!"

I'm torn. Should I run away, or check what's happening? I don't hesitate for long. I creep back the way I came, so I can glimpse the action through the trees.

Two men have Freya by the arms.

Eugene stands in front of her, looking taller than I remember. "Care to explain why you have Jamie's smart band?"

"We had a bet. I lost, so I had to do his run today."

"You're lying. Where is he?"

The man slaps Freya hard across the face. I wonder what happened to the idea that physical violence is always wrong.

Freya lets out a small sob. "He went in the other direction."

"What do you mean?"

"Jamie said his uncle told him to go to the yellow zone. And he asked me to come this way in case you were tracking his band."

She's doing her best to throw them off the scent.

Eugene is no fool. He's calculating the probabilities. "Did he say why he was going there?"

"Something about the vaccine. He plans to destroy it."

She's come up with a motive that even Eugene can believe.

"I see. You've been most helpful."

"Shall we release her?" asks one of the men.

"No, she already knows too much. Take her to the detention block. And make sure she stays silent."

"You can't do this," shouts Freya, but the man clamps his hand over her mouth as they drag her away.

I want to run to her aid, but there's nothing I can do.

Besides, Freya might be in trouble, but she's not about to die, unlike the rest of the population. I need to focus on the task in hand, or Freya's sacrifice will be for nothing.

I jog back into the woods.

The green zone is miles away, on the other side of the lake. Old Man Devlin's cabin is further still.

I have a long journey ahead.

And I'm running out of time.

TWENTY-SEVEN

It takes hours.

I stumble through the undergrowth, tripping up roots. I've left the path behind. The place Freya pointed to on the map is deep in a valley, and there are no tracks to follow. I guess that's to discourage anyone from coming this way.

As I head further down, the ground becomes boggy. I do my best to avoid the largest puddles, the mud sucking at my trainers as I run.

I'm shattered, but I force myself on.

There's no time to rest, no time to think. Only one thing matters: I have to find a way out of Arcadia so I can warn the Resistance about Plan B. That means I have to convince Old Man Devlin to help, assuming he's not as crazy as Freya made out. Otherwise, I'm dead.

People exaggerate, right?

He probably just got sick of living in a close-knit community. I could understand that. If I lived here for any length of time, the pace of life in Arcadia would drive me mad. Who wouldn't want to get away from it all?

The sun might be out, but the forest is gloomy. The canopy of trees blocks out most of the light. I come to a stream and I double-check the map.

Before the lockdown, maps were a mystery to me, but during my time in the Resistance, I learnt how to use them. Kieran and I were runners, and we had to use old maps to get around. The Quarantine Agency would have traced us if we used anything digital. I'm glad of those skills now. Out here, in the middle of the forest, there's very little to go on. I know roughly where I am, but I can't work out if I've wandered too far north.

Come on, Zac. Get it together.

I take a running jump over the stream, landing neatly on the other side. I glance in both directions, wondering whether to head left or right. Truthfully, Old Man Devlin's cabin could be either way.

Something catches my eye. A piece of fur, hanging on a tree. I cautiously creep towards it.

It's a fox. A dead one. All its blood has drained out, and it looks like it's been here for some time, nailed to the trunk. Flies buzz around the sorry-looking corpse.

Why would someone do that?

As I look around, my heart stops.

There are more. A badger. A bird. A squirrel. Some other creatures that I can't even identify. It's like an animal graveyard, but nothing's been buried.

Are you still sure Old Man Devlin isn't crazy?

I'm miles from civilisation, in a creepy forest, surrounded by dead animals. I want to run. But I'm on a mission and I'm not about to turn back. I push on, trying to ignore the growing sense of dread.

Now, there are signs. They appear to be painted by hand in red paint. At least, I hope that's what it is.

"KEEP OUT OR DIE."

I wonder if Old Man Devlin will nail me up with the animals after he's killed me. It's not a pleasant thought.

I'm still thinking about that when I get one hell of a shock.

It happens so fast, I don't know what's going on. There's a whooshing noise and I shoot up into the air. I find myself dangling from a tree, caught in a net. The ropes tighten around me, forcing my body into a ball. I try to push my way out, but the weight of my body holds the net closed. There's no way out of this, not without a knife. Sadly, I didn't bring one of those.

Besides, the ground looks a long way down. Even if I could climb out, I don't fancy falling that distance.

What, then?

I really only have one option. I shout as loud as I can, hoping that Old Man Devlin will hear: "HELP! HELP!"

No one comes.

I keep calling, but it's hopeless.

After a while, I stop. My throat is sore and I can't keep it up forever.

I contemplate the grim possibility that I could die up here. What if no one knows I'm here and no one ever checks?

I'd die of hunger and thirst, or maybe

exposure. But that would take a long time.

I push against the net, sheer desperation giving me strength. But it's no good. I'm curled up small, my face pressed against my knees.

And all I can do is wait.

***

I don't know how long it takes.

What I do know is that the net feels even tighter than before. I can hardly breathe.

"You got a death wish, boy?"

I twist around as much as I can, so I can see who's speaking. It's an old guy, the oldest I've seen in Arcadia by far. His long straggly grey hair falls past his shoulders, looking like it's never been combed, and his beard reaches his waist. He's dressed in a dirty checked shirt and blue jeans. The shirt hangs open at the front, showing a yellow vest that probably used to be white.

"Well?" he demands. "You mute as well as stupid?"

"No, sir. I'm afraid I got caught in your trap."

He snorts. "That's what it's for."

To my horror, he starts to walk away.

"Hey, you can't just leave me here."

"Can't I?" He doesn't appear to care. I wonder if he's just messing with me, but there's something wild in his eyes. This man has been out in the woods too long.

I don't even try to hide the desperation in my voice. "If you do, I'll die."

He shrugs. "We all die. Some sooner than others. You should have paid attention to the signs."

If he gets any further away, he won't be able to hear me. I have to convince him to let me out now, or I may not get another chance.

"Aaron sent me."

That makes him stop. He turns to face me, but his face is screwed up, even uglier than before. "Aaron Greaves? He told you to come here?"

"Yes, sir." It's not strictly true, but this isn't the time to quibble about details.

If he's one of the founders, he must know Aaron really well. I'm hoping they're friends.

It turns out, they're not.

The old man's face looks even meaner than before.

"If that's true, then I should kill you myself."

TWENTY-EIGHT

He stalks off into the forest.

I call after him, worried that I've blown it.

How was I meant to know that Old Man Devlin hates Aaron?

And what else can I say that will convince him to let me down?

"They're going to launch Plan B!" I yell. He's so far away by now, I'm not even sure he can hear me.

If he does, it doesn't make a difference. He keeps walking. I'm left in his trap, wondering if he'll leave me here to rot.

Surely, he wouldn't do that?

The man is seriously unhinged. I wouldn't put it past him.

As I hang, the frustration builds. Every minute

matters. The longer I'm trapped, the less time I have to escape from Arcadia and warn the Resistance. Truthfully, it looks like that plan is already in tatters.

I start thinking about the people outside. I think about my mum and my brother who were taken into quarantine. I wonder if they're ok, and how long it will be before they catch the virus once Plan B is rolled out. I always thought I'd see them again.

And then there are all my friends in the Resistance: Kieran, Trix, Sayeed, Del and the others. They'll all be dead in a few months. I've failed them. Not only did I never get them access to the Collective network, but I haven't even managed to warn them about the fake vaccine.

Tears pour down my cheeks, and I don't make any attempt to wipe them away. It's too hard in the confines of the net and there's no point. I need to grieve for my family and friends; to mourn the millions of people who will lose their lives.

They're all about to die, because of me.

"You might want to try to relax."

The voice startles me. I've been so caught up

in my own emotion that I didn't hear Old Man Devlin return. I wonder if he's here to free me. But then I see something which steals that hope away.

He's loading a gun.

"What?" I'm so afraid, I can barely speak.

"You look tense. Try to relax." He finishes putting in the bullets, then lifts the rifle on to his shoulder and points it at me.

"You want me to relax?" I repeat it back to him, hoping that some shred of humanity remains.

"If you don't, this is really going to hurt."

Just how crazy is this man?

"Yeah? I have a feeling it might hurt anyway. So, go ahead. Shoot."

As I say it, I realise I mean it.

Why should I get to live when everyone else doesn't?

My self-pity is lost on Old Man Devlin. If I was hoping for some comforting words, or for him to put down the gun, then I'm soon disappointed.

"Suit yourself," he says.

A grin stretches across his face as he starts to squeeze the trigger.

He's going to kill me, and he's happy about it.

I close my eyes and prepare for the end.

***

He fires.

The sound of the rifle cuts through the forest like the crack of a whip.

Time stops. I wait for the pain to register, for my body to scream in agony, for the blood to flow. I wonder where I'll feel it, whether he aimed for my head or my chest. At least if he put a bullet through my brain, I won't know about it for long.

But there's nothing.

He missed.

Either that or this is just some insane game he likes to play with his victims.

Another shot, and the same storm of emotions. I've lost control of my senses. I just want this to be over.

Still, nothing.

Now, I'm angry. Furious, in fact.

"What are you waiting for? Just do it! Come on!"

"Quiet, boy. I'm trying my best. You just try to

relax, like I told you."

As far as I'm concerned, the conversation couldn't get any more surreal.

Come on, Zac. Just relax while the old man shoots you.

I almost laugh out loud at the absurdity of it.

The third shot hits something. I feel a vibration in the net and wonder if the bullet has cut through one of the strands before puncturing my defenceless body.

Still, there's no pain.

There is, however, a new sense of fear.

Because without warning, the net begins to fall.

***

I drop to the ground like a stone, landing with an almighty splash in a deep muddy puddle. Adrenaline numbs my senses. My face is pressed into the water. The net is tangled around me, but now it's no longer hanging, I find that I can pull it free. I clamber out, covered in mud, coughing and spluttering.

"You alright?" asks Old Man Devlin. He's still

holding the rifle, but it's no longer pointing at me.

"I-I-I think so."

"Come with me."

With that, he strides into the woods.

I fall in step behind him, not entirely sure if the danger has passed. I guess if he wanted to kill me, he'd have done it already. But death isn't the only unpleasant thing that can happen to a kid.

"Why'd you come here, boy?"

"Zac. My name is Zac."

"That's not what I asked."

I don't know how much to tell him, but there doesn't seem to be much point holding back. "They took Aaron away. Eugene and some other men. And they're talking about Plan B."

"Talking about it, or doing it?"

"Doing it. That's why they need Aaron out of the way."

"I bet they do," he mumbles. "Still, I don't see why this involves me."

I look up at him, my eyes pleading. "I need to get out of Arcadia, to take a message to someone. It's the only way to stop the Collective wiping everyone out."

"And you think that's a bad thing?"

"Yeah. Don't you?"

"I don't know what I think any more. I just want everyone to leave me alone." He holds his head as he says it, as if talking to me is causing him physical pain.

"I will. I promise. I just need you to tell me if there's a way out."

"Oh, there's a way out. But you won't like it."

TWENTY-NINE

My mind is made up. "I'll do whatever it takes."

"We'll see."

We walk towards a cabin. It's much more basic than the ones in the red zone. The door creaks as it opens, and even though I'm short, I have to duck as I step inside.

A sparse bed sits in one corner, with a cupboard nearby. At the other end is a table which seems to double as a kitchen worktop. There are a couple of chairs and some kind of stove. There are no other rooms. I don't even want to know where the old man goes to the toilet, but the whole place smells of sweat and stagnant swamp. I try not to show my disgust.

"Have a seat," he says, pulling out a chair.

I obediently drop into it. "Why did you leave?

I mean, why didn't you stay close to everyone else?"

"Politics." He almost spits the word. "Once the senate was formed, everything got decided by a stupid committee. Before you knew it, people had to wear the same clothes and no one could eat meat. A bunch of vegans running the place! Can you imagine?"

I don't need to imagine. I've seen it. "So, you left?"

"I mind my own business and they leave me alone. That's the deal." He glances over to me. "At least, that's how it's *meant* to work."

"Hey, you tell me how to get out of this place and I'm gone. Quick as a flash." I'm not lying. I can't wait to get away, before he decides he'd rather eat me than help me escape. "You know any way out of here."

"Well, there's a tunnel. The entrance is hidden, but it leads under the fences to the outside."

I feel hope rising up in me. That doesn't sound too bad. "Where is it?"

The man shakes his head, sadly. "It doesn't matter. You can't use it."

"Why not?"

"Eugene knows about it. All the founders do. If he's about to put Plan B into action, he won't take any risks. He'll have the entrance guarded day and night. Or he'll have it blocked off."

I want to object, but Old Man Devlin is right. Eugene doesn't strike me as the kind of guy who takes chances. If he's sent people looking for me, he'll have also made sure I can't get out of Arcadia.

"So, it's hopeless." I let out a long sigh.

He holds up his hand.

At first, I think he's silencing me because he's just had a genius idea.

But then I hear it myself, a noise outside. There's a faint buzzing and the sound of voices in the distance.

"Get under the bed." He grabs me by my arm and pushes me across the room. I dive to the floor and slide under. I find myself lying on a thick layer of dust, and I have to share the space with a crusty old handkerchief and an old woollen sock.

Old Man Devlin might not be concerned about the cleanliness of his hut, but he sure likes to keep it secure. I peer out as he opens a cupboard and pulls out a large gun. He checks it's loaded, then throws open the door and stands in the entrance.

"Get the hell off my land," he yells. "If any of you take one step closer, I'll blow your brains out."

Someone speaks back. They're using some form of loudspeaker or PA system. "Put the gun down, Devlin. You're surrounded. We're all armed, but we'd rather not shoot you."

"Yeah? Then why are you here?"

"We've come for the boy. We know he came looking for you. Return him to us and we'll leave you in peace. Otherwise, we'll kill you and take him."

For a moment, I'm worried. They're offering him the peace and quiet he so desperately wants. But, fortunately, Old Man Devlin has principles.

"I don't take kindly to threats, and I don't know nothing about no boy. So, get yourselves off my land while you still have the chance."

"Don't be ridiculous, Devlin. What are you going to do against six soldiers and three drones?"

The old man is ranting like a lunatic. "Ha! You think you're clever, coming here with your fancy lasers and your flying machines?"

"I think you'd be crazy to try to get in our way."

"Let's see, shall we?" Old Man Devlin fumbles in his pocket. He pulls out a small cylinder, around the size of a pen. It has a red button at one end. "What do you think will happen if I press this button?"

No smart responses from the guy outside this time. I don't know if he's worried, or whether he's given up trying to reason with the old man.

It doesn't matter. Devlin presses the button and something happens. I feel it as much as hear it. THUD. THUD. THUD.

"Looks like your drones need a rest."

"What did you do, Devlin?" There's no amplification now. Just the shouted words of an angry man.

"Electro-magnetic pulse. Everything electrical within five hundred yards has been neutralised. I sure hope it hasn't affected your lasers." At this, he pulls back on the shotgun and lifts it to his shoulder. "Of course, old-fashioned guns such as these don't need any circuit boards or batteries.

Nothing but a well-oiled mechanism and a small trigger. Want me to show you how it works?"

Silence.

"Hey, where are you going? Leaving so soon?" Devlin is enjoying himself now. "What happened to all those empty threats?"

I can just about make out the men's last words. "We'll come back, Devlin. And you'll pay for this."

"I told you I don't take kindly to threats."

Without warning, he fires the gun. I don't know if he's aiming at them or not, but no more noise comes from the forest.

As soon as they're gone, he beckons me out from under the bed. "You're a right pain in the ass, you know that?"

"You're not the first to say it. Why didn't you hand me over?"

"I might've. If they'd asked nicely." There's a twinkle in his eye. I think he's joking. "I've had enough of Eugene telling the rest of us what to do."

I get the impression he cares more about that than about all the people who will die if Plan B is put into action. Still, I'll take what I can get.

"Thanks for not selling me out."

"It's not over yet. We have to get you out of here, before they come back with something I can't neutralise with the EMP."

"It's pointless. You said it yourself. If they've blocked the tunnel, I'll never get out of Arcadia."

"No, boy. I never said that was the *only* way out. But now they know you're here, we need to move fast."

"The faster the better," I say. "What exactly do you have in mind?"

"I'm going to teach you to fly."

THIRTY

Of course you are.

I shouldn't be surprised.

Everyone told me Old Man Devlin was nuts, and he certainly seems a few cards short of a full deck. But then, he's been wily enough to fight off the soldiers and drones that were sent to capture me. Perhaps he's not as crazy as he appears?

"You're going to teach me to fly?" I repeat if back to him, watching my tone. He might be as mad as a hatter, but he's my only ally right now, and I don't want to offend him. "How?"

"Flap your arms, boy. Really fast."

I swallow hard. I'm not sure how to respond to that.

A broad smile breaks across his face, his wrinkles deepening like cracks in an earthquake.

"Ha! You thought I was serious."

"Maybe," I admit. "So, I'm not going to fly?"

"Oh, you are. Just not like that. You're going to use a little invention of mine." He leads me out of the cabin and into the woods. He moves surprisingly fast for an old guy and I struggle to keep up. "I have to keep things hidden, in case the tide turns."

I'm guessing he's talking about the political landscape in Arcadia, rather than the ocean. "I think it just did."

"You're not wrong."

We're silent for a while as we push our way through the undergrowth. I swear as thorns scratch at my arms and legs.

That makes Devlin laugh. "Are those fancy futuristic clothes not offering you much protection?"

"Hey, I didn't choose to wear these," I point out. "These are the only clothes they have, back in the red zone."

"Then it's a good job I got out when I did. Here we are."

Devlin is standing between the trees. There's no sign of a cabin or shed or anything else. I'm beginning to wonder if his inventions are all in his imagination and whether this whole expedition is futile. But he reaches down and brushes soil and leaves aside, revealing a hatch.

He pulls it up, letting it fall back with a massive thud. I look down at the square hole. A ladder leads into the blackness.

"Go on, then," says Devlin, gesturing to it. "Get down there."

I hesitate. I have no way of knowing if this underground bunker is full of his inventions or whether it's a prison he uses to torture anyone who trespasses on his land. But what choice do I have? He's had plenty of opportunities to kill me already. I have to trust him, crazy or not.

Slowly, I make my way down. He follows behind. If I'm honest, I'm relieved that he hasn't slammed the hatch shut as soon as I'm inside.

Before long, my foot hits something hard. The floor. I reach around but can't feel anything.

"Just step back and let me down," he orders.

As he steps off the ladder, he reaches to his left and flips a switch. The lights flicker on. We're standing in an underground container, about the size of a truck. Shelves line the walls, full of half-finished gadgets and bundles of electrical cable. One wall is lined with guns, but I'm more interested in the stack of tins in the corner. I pick one up. Some kind of canned fruit.

"You hungry, boy?"

I nod.

He takes the tin and rummages around for an opener. The device he uses tears the lid off, leaving a jagged edge. He hands me a spoon. It doesn't look clean, but I don't want to seem ungrateful, so I just dive in.

"This is good," I say, enjoying the taste of the sickly sweet syrup. "How did you get all of this down here?"

"This bunker was here before Arcadia was built," he says. "I lived on this land before anyone else. Before Aaron convinced me to join him on his fool's errand to save the world."

"If you help me, we might still have a chance."

"Huh. We'll see."

He wanders over to one of the shelves and starts muttering to himself as he sorts through the junk. "Valve... hose... tank... fabric..." He picks up an enormous sheet and drops it on the floor. It's silver and shiny, and I can't help wondering what it's for.

"This invention of yours. What is it exactly?"

"A mini-zeppelin."

I look at him, confused.

"A bit like a hot-air balloon," he explains. "It uses gas instead of a burner. Don't they teach you anything in school?"

"I guess not."

"We need to get this lot up there." He points to the roof. "Then we'll put it all together. See if she flies."

I don't like the sound of that last part. "Haven't you used it before?"

He snorts. "Nope. Help me carry this to the ladder."

I haul the equipment piece by piece, tripping over the shiny canvas as it keeps slipping out of my hands.

"Careful with that," he warns. "One rip and the whole plan is doomed."

"Good to know." I carefully gather up the trailing fabric and take smaller steps towards the base of the ladder. "How are we going to get it up there?"

"In this." He grabs a wicker basket and starts

to pile the stuff in. Before long, Devlin has found some ropes and tied them around the handles of the basket.

"Want me to go up the ladder and pull it up?" I ask.

He shakes his head. "You wouldn't stand a chance. We'll do it together."

I try not to feel insulted as I climb the ladder behind him, then pass up the ends of the ropes. As soon as we're above ground, and we start to pull, I see what he means. It's surprisingly heavy.

Beads of sweat form on my forehead. I want to stop and have a rest, but there's no way to do that, and my pride won't let me admit defeat. So, instead, I tug harder, relieved when the basket is high enough for us to haul it out with the last of our strength.

I no longer care what Devlin thinks. As soon as it's on the ground, I collapse, exhausted.

He's made of much tougher stuff. While I rest, he gets to work, piecing the equipment together in a small clearing, a short distance from the hatch. He clamps the rubber tubing on to the gas tank. There are some cords that have been sewn into the shiny fabric, and he fastens these to the corners of the basket.

"You can use this to stand in," he says.

I gulp. The basket won't even reach to my waist. "I can't go up in that. I'll fall out."

"Best sit down, then."

He fiddles around for ages, tightening this and fastening that. I'm not going to complain. The last thing I want to do is distract him when he's making sure everything is safe. Not that it *looks* very safe. It has all the design features of a hot-air balloon from the nineteen-forties.

"Take a look at this," he says, and I head over. "When you want to go up, you release more gas from the tank by turning this valve."

"And if I want to go down?"

"Then you pull these two cords here. But be careful. They'll bring you down fast."

"How do I steer?"

"You don't. You let the wind take you."

"What if it's in the wrong direction?"

"There is no wrong direction. You go up and the wind carries you one way or another. Eventually you'll cross the fences on one side of the compound. Then you come down."

I suddenly feel very alone. "Can't you come

with me?"

"This isn't a group outing, kid. It won't carry two of us. Too much weight."

"But I-"

He holds up a hand to silence me. I think it's because he doesn't want me to argue, but as I shut up, I hear something.

Voices in the distance.

The men are coming back.

THIRTY-ONE

The old man swears under his breath.

"What do we do?" I hiss.

"Hide in the bunker. I'll try to head them off. As soon as it's dark, you inflate the zeppelin and escape. You hear me?"

He pushes me towards the hatch, then picks up his shotgun and pushes his way back through the forest.

Fear grips me. I've lost control of my body. I stand, rooted to the spot, not sure whether I can face going back underground. Maybe I should follow Old Man Devlin and see what happens? I need to know whether he lives or dies.

No, that's a stupid idea. It's a surefire way to get caught. I'm some distance from the cabin. The men have no reason to come all the way out here. Best to stick to the plan.

I cautiously climb back down the ladder and close the hatch. Before I click it into place, I make sure there's a way to open it from the inside. There is. Old Man Devlin isn't stupid enough to risk getting trapped in his own bunker.

What now?

I sit in an old rusty chair and stroke my legs, trying to get them to stop shaking. I'm so close to getting out of here. I can't mess this up.

Why did the old man tell me to wait until it was dark before I used the zeppelin? I guess someone would see if it flew over the settlements in Arcadia. Or maybe he was more worried about the people on the outside, who are still in lockdown? Anyone who spotted an aircraft would report it.

But the longer the zeppelin is out there, the more chance there is that one of Eugene's men will find it. No option is risk-free.

The stress makes me hungry and I help myself to some more tins of food. I don't know if Devlin will go mad when he finds out, but it's not like he's running short on supplies. Besides, right now that's the last of my worries.

I can't just sit here. I have to know what's happening.

The guns on the wall are a mystery to me. Even in the Resistance, I wasn't allowed a firearm. I have no idea how any of them work. Still, I feel safer taking one. I might be able to bluff my way out of danger.

Slowly, I climb the ladder with it. When I reach the top, I ease open the hatch. It's still daylight, but I can't see or hear the men, so I slide out, lowering the cover back into place. Then, I steal forwards, towards the clearing where we left the zeppelin.

It's still there. I was so sure they'd have found it and taken it away that I want to cry for joy when I see the silvery fabric lying on the ground, next to the wicker basket.

What now?

Should I take it for a ride, or wait it out?

I'm about to creep over when I see something that stops me in my tracks. A man is approaching the zeppelin, a gun slung over his shoulder. He's speaking into a radio.

"Still no sign of the boy, but I've found something really strange. Looks like some sort of hot-air balloon."

There's a crackle and hiss and someone says something on the other end. I can't make out the words, but whatever his colleague says makes the man laugh. "Roger that. The old man will have one hell of a headache when he wakes up. I'll stay here until you arrive. I think the boss will want to see this himself."

Now, I have no choice. If I wait any longer, it's game over. I have to go now. And I have to get rid of the man before anyone else appears.

Use the gun.

That's my first thought, and it's stupid.

I don't want to kill him. And I couldn't shoot him, even if I wanted to. I don't know how to load the gun or release the safety. Besides, he has a weapon of his own. The minute he realises I don't have a clue what I'm doing, I'm dead.

What, then?

Whatever I'm going to do, it'd better be quick.

I glance back at the hatch and have a flash of an idea. I have no idea if it will work, but I don't have time to think it through.

Cautiously, I open the bunker. Then I step back, throw down the gun I'm holding, and dive into a nearby bush. There's a loud clang as the gun hits the floor of the container. With any luck, the man will hear it.

Sure enough, less than a minute later, he appears, his gun cocked. His eyes search the greenery and I wonder if he'll spot me before he sees the open hatch. Fortunately, he sees the black hole first and steps towards it, pointing his gun into the darkness.

"Is anyone down there?" he shouts.

He waits a bit, unsure whether to proceed or wait for backup. If he decides to wait it out, then I'm in trouble. My plan won't work.

Thankfully, his curiosity gets the better of him and he takes hold of the ladder, making his way down. I want to slam the hatch shut, but that will give the game away. Before I do that, there's something else I need to do.

I dash over to the zeppelin and turn the valve on the gas tank to the on position. This plan is stupid; it's never going to work. But now, I hardly have a choice.

Better to go down fighting.

I dart back across to the bunker and peer in. The man has found the light switch. Now he's sure the place is empty, he's lowered his gun and is examining the food with interest. Suddenly, he looks up. Our eyes meet.

"Stay right there," he says, like he's in any position to give orders.

He hurries up the ladder. If I don't stop him, he'll be out in seconds.

I wait until he's about to come out, but just as his hands reach the top, I stamp down, giving him a brutal blow to the face. I hear him cry out and fall back. Then, I slam shut the hatch and sit on it, wondering if my body weight will be enough to trap him.

I have to hope it will, because when I glance over at the zeppelin, the fabric is still lying on the ground. It's starting to inflate, but it'll take some time to fill up completely.

And time is something I don't have.

I can hear angry shouts from the container below. My prisoner pushes up with such force that it almost knocks me off the hatch. I grip the handle and push my backside down with all my might, trying to hold it shut. I might be lightweight, but gravity is on my side. After a nervous few minutes, the shouts subside and the man stops pushing. He's probably hoping I'll give up. After all, I can't sit on the hatch forever.

Besides, he knows his buddies will be here soon to rescue him.

The silvery fabric ripples and starts to lift into the air. One side of it is trying to drag the rest skyward and I wonder at what point the basket will lift off the ground. The moment it does, I have to make a run for it. But I wonder if I can cover the distance in time to dive in, or whether it will already be too high.

If I get off the hatch too early, the man will get out and stop me. If I leave it too late, the zeppelin will fly away without me.

You're screwed either way.

More pushing from underneath, and I can also hear some voices in the distance.

"Hank? Where are you? Your signal's weak."

They'll be here any second.

The other half of the fabric is in the air now, and the cables grow tight. It still doesn't look all that likely that the thing will ever fly. The balloon's not that big and the basket looks so big and heavy.

"HANK!"

They're close now. I glimpse movement through the trees.

There's one more push on the hatch. This one catches me off guard and sends me stumbling sideways. Hank forces it open and pulls himself up. There's a look of pure rage on his blood-smeared face. It looks like I broke his nose with my kick.

"Now you're gonna get it!" he yells, scrambling out of the bunker.

I sprint across the clearing, the man hot on my heels.

He dives, tackling me to the ground. I lash out, kicking hard, then pull away. I'm back on my feet, running for dear life towards the zeppelin.

It's in the air. The basket is rising off the ground.

With the last of my energy, I leap, my hands grabbing the sides. That brings it down a few feet, my body weight pulling against the zeppelin's movement. It's enough to let me scramble in.

"STOP HIM!"

More men are running over. One of them tries to grab the basket, but he's too late. The balloon is fully inflated now, and the zeppelin is picking up speed, rising at an alarming rate towards the tree-tops.

"Shoot it!" shouts one of the men.

One rip and the whole plan is doomed.

That's what Old Man Devlin said. If they put a bullet through the fabric, I'm going to drop back to earth like a stone.

As I peer over the edge of the basket, I can see a man lifting up a rifle and pointing it towards the zeppelin.

He's going to fire.

And it's a long way to fall.

THIRTY-TWO

I slide down inside the basket and let out a loud groan.

There's a deafening crack as the man fires the gun. I look up to see if I can spot the damage. There's a small hole in the bottom of the zeppelin. There must be one on top as well, where the bullet came out.

Despite that, I'm still rising, much more quickly than I expect. If he shoots again, that won't last for long.

I cower down, waiting for the inevitable.

It doesn't come.

There are no more gunshots.

Why would they stop?

I force myself to peer over the side. Then, I wish I hadn't. I'm so high up, I feel sick. My whole body shakes. The zeppelin is being blown across the forest. I can't even see the men; there are too many trees in the way.

You did it!

I know I should be happy that I've escaped, but this is no time to celebrate.

It's freezing up here. Even the active wear can't compensate for the icy wind. I want to huddle in the basket and hug my knees and wait for this nightmare to be over, but I can't.

I have to try to get my bearings so I know when I've crossed the boundary and I'm finally free of Arcadia. Then, I have to work out how to land this thing and find a way to contact the Resistance.

My life is like a long to-do list where every task is impossible.

Suck it up, Zac.

I check out the view in each direction. The lake is behind me. That's good news. I'm heading away from the Arcadian settlements, which means there's less chance anyone will spot me. That being said, it's still daylight and people aren't used to seeing aircraft in lockdown. I can't imagine I'll avoid detection for long.

The wind takes me along the valley between the steep hills. A stream runs between them and in the far distance I can see a small town. If I make it there, I might find a computer.

I force myself to look down, even though it makes my head spin. A short distance in front of me, I can make out the line of the fence. Beyond it are some metal posts, spread apart like metal sentinels. Those must be the motion detectors. Then, a solid metal barrier. Looks like Freya was right. The bolt-cutters would have been useless.

Now, though, I should be able to sail over the lot.

The fences get closer.

Too close, in fact.

I realise I'm losing altitude.

Frantically, I check the tank. It's almost empty. The gas is slowly escaping through the holes in the fabric. I'm going to land soon, whether I like it or not.

I'm all for having my feet back on the ground, but only once I'm across both fences. As things stand, it looks like I'll touch down in the no-man's-land between them. If I do that, I'll get zapped by the lasers.

Please, no.

There's nothing I can throw overboard to lighten the load. Well, nothing except the empty gas tank. I do that, but it makes zero difference. The zeppelin is billowing above me, feeling less stable by the second. I think one of the bullet holes has become a tear. Meanwhile, the solid steel fence is right in front of me, its top adorned with spikes. If I can just get past it, I know I'll be fine. There's a last gust of wind that brings me hope. Sadly, it's not to be. The basket crashes into the fence, jarring me so hard I almost topple over the side.

The rest of the zeppelin carries on a bit further, the cords getting trapped between the spikes. It can't pull the basket over or break free. It billows hopelessly, descending further. Before long, the silvery fabric hangs down the other side of the fence, deflated and useless.

It's a precarious situation to be in.

The remains of the zeppelin are hanging over the top of the steel fence. The basket is lopsided, and if I move, it threatens to capsize and tip me out. I may not be as high as I was a few moments ago, but I'm still a long way up. If I fall, I die.

What now, Zac?

There are no handholds, no way down. Even if I could lower myself to the ground below, I'd be caught in the danger zone, unable to move without triggering the motion detectors.

I have to get over this fence if it kills me.

Which it probably will.

The only hope I have is to use the cords of the zeppelin to haul myself over, and then try to climb down the fabric on the other side.

I grab hold of the cords. Even that motion makes the basket move under my feet. I'm terrified. Any moment now, it could fall away.

That's why you have to do this. Get a grip.

I smile weakly at my own joke and take a deep breath. Then, I go for it. I cling to the cord, pulling my body up, inch by inch. The rope burns into my flesh, making my hands sore. A few more feet and I can grab hold of the top of the fence and haul myself over. Even that's harder than it looks. I have to grip the narrow spikes in my fist and try to push my body over. By the time I'm on the other side, I have a deep scratch on my thigh which almost extends to my privates.

I'm exhausted. The effort of holding on is too

much. But the fear of falling is even greater. If I drop from this height, I'll break both my legs, or worse. Somehow, I have to ease myself down the cords towards the hanging fabric, then use that as a kind of makeshift rope the rest of the way to the ground.

I manage to ease my way further down, but it turns out the fabric is much more slippery than I expect. Even when I try to gather it tightly and grip hard, I can't hold on for long.

There's a terrible moment when I know it's over.

The silvery sheet slips from my hands.

And I start to fall.

THIRTY-THREE

Impact.

I expect the ground to be hard, but instead it's soft and prickly. A thorn bush. I might get scratched to pieces but I'm just glad I don't feel the snap of any bones. Even landing in the bush has left me bumped and bruised, my limbs catching on thick branches.

I swear. Loudly.

I can't remember the last time so many parts of my body hurt at the same time.

Pushing my way out is difficult. I feel like I'm swimming through barbed wire. Eventually, I stumble on to moss-covered ground.

My breath comes in sharp gasps. I can't get enough oxygen. My heart is battering my chest like a machine gun.

I've nearly died. More than once.

And this isn't over.

The sun is getting lower. There are only a few hours of daylight left. If I'm going to reach the town I saw, I have to move fast. Besides, Eugene and his men know I've escaped. They'll probably come after me. I can't hang around.

Wheezing, I try to jog down the valley. I can see the stream. If I reach that. I can follow it all the way to the town. One of my legs hurts every time I put any weight on it, but that can't be helped.

I'm just starting to calm down and tell myself the worst is over when I hear dogs barking in the distance, followed by men shouting. There's only one reason anyone would be out here with dogs. They're hunting me like a fox.

Get moving, Zac.

There's no way I'll reach the stream before they catch me. I wonder whether the men will restrain the hounds, or whether they'll let them tear me to pieces with their teeth. I don't even have the energy to feel afraid any more. I've used up all the adrenaline my body can produce. Now, I just feel tired.

Hysteria takes a hold of me. I can go no further.

The barks are getting louder.

"I give up. I surrender." I try to shout it, but my voice comes out much quieter than I expect.

I can't even hand myself in without making a mess of it. Tears stream down my cheeks.

I say it again, this time a bit louder. "I'm over here. I surrender."

"Oh no, you don't."

Someone grabs me from behind. A gloved hand clamps over my mouth, preventing me from speaking and I'm dragged backwards behind a bush.

That voice. I know that voice.

Kieran.

He spins me round and I find myself looking up at him. His face is smeared with dirt and he's wearing the army gear that we were given when we joined the Resistance.

"Are you real?" I can't help but wonder if I'm hallucinating. To see my best friend here, right at my moment of greatest need, feels too good to be true.

"Am I real? Heck, Zac, have you gone insane?

And what are you wearing? Did you become a superhero or join a cycling club?"

I look down at my ruined Arcadia uniform. "It looked better before it got ripped."

"I'll take your word for it. We have to go." He pulls me along a muddy path to a cluster of trees.

Kieran might be here, but so are the dogs. I can see them in the distance running towards us. They'll be on us in no time.

"We'll never outrun them," I say. "I can't even walk properly."

"Good job I brought this then." Kieran reaches behind a tree and pulls out a dirt bike. He tosses me a helmet. "I think you need this more than I do."

"Thanks." I pull it on.

He smiles again. "Just for the record, you look like an idiot."

I've missed his insults. "Good to know."

"Jump on." He sits on the bike and gestures to the back. Then, he kicks the starter, and the engine fires up. It sounds stupidly loud.

"Won't they hear us?" I say.

"Course they will. But they'll never catch us."

With that, we're off. A cloud of dirt shoots up

behind, so big that it showers some of the dogs with dirt as they break through the trees. Kieran opens the throttle and we power over the uneven ground, jumping and sliding like we're at a rally. I cling to his waist like a little kid.

"How did you find me?" I ask.

"We've been keeping an eye on Arcadia, ever since you went there. It wasn't difficult to spot a giant silver balloon trying to make an escape. They told me to come and get you."

"Thanks for the rescue," I shout, over the sound of the motor. "I thought I was done for."

"Yeah, well you're not out of the woods yet."

His words steal some of my elation. For a moment, I think he means that there's still the possibility we'll get caught. But then I realise he said *you're* not *we're*. It's me that's in trouble, not him.

"What do you mean?" I shout.

"Layla is *not* happy. You were gone for weeks and didn't hack their systems. She's gonna give you a whipping when you get back."

"Layla can go swivel," I mutter. "I nearly died in there. It wasn't as easy as she thinks."

"Yeehaa!" says Kieran, as we shoot over a

bump, flying through the air. "That's the spirit, Zac. We're gonna make a proper rebel out of you yet!"

I want to smile, but I'm too tired to even do that. All I can do is hold on, and hope that it's enough.

EPILOGUE

I always think it's going to get better.

It never does.

I go from one ordeal to another.

I'm carrying a secret so terrible, no one will believe me. I don't even know if I'm on the right side. If I tell the Resistance about the vaccine being poisoned, they might be able to stop it being released. But at what cost? What if the Collective are right and wiping out the majority of the population is the only way that any of us will survive?

No. I have to do this. I have to stop them.

But first, I have to warn the Resistance that their cover has been blown. If Layla is already mad at me, she'll go nuclear when she hears that. Especially when she finds out it's all my fault.

Then, I need to tell them everything else I know.

That's if they'll listen.

And if I even get back to headquarters without being caught.

My name is Zac, and I'm a member of the Resistance.

At least, I was, before I screwed up this mission.

Now, they'll never trust me again.

FIND OUT WHAT HAPPENS NEXT:

They have a plan.

He has to stop them.

He'll need the Resistance to help. But it's not easy to convince them of the truth when everyone thinks you're a traitor.

Caught between rival factions, Zac doesn't know who to trust.

Time is running out and his enemies are closing in.

If he fails, everyone will die.

Including him.

Want to know when it's released? Sign up to my reader's club for updates, free books and more!

Check out www.paulorton.net for more details.

A NOTE FROM THE AUTHOR

Thanks for reading *The Call of the Collective*. I'll soon be releasing the next book in the Lockdown series: *The Fall of Freedom*. If you want to be kept informed when it's released then check out www.paulorton.net.

You may also want to get hold of my other books: the *Ryan Jacobs* series. If you like teenagers with attitude, you'll love Ryan Jacobs! You can even download the prequel to the series completely free on my website.

But first, could you do me a huge favour? I'd love you to review *The Call of the Collective* on Amazon. Reviews make a huge difference to an independent author like me, and it would be amazing if you could write a sentence or two about what you liked about it. I'd really appreciate it and I promise I read <u>every</u> review.

Until next time,

Paul.

GET YOUR FREE EBOOK

There are traps you can't escape.

When Ryan Jacobs asks to join the Faction he finds himself trapped in a situation which keeps getting worse. He needs to escape fast, or they will own him forever. But how can he fight an invisible enemy?

Find out about Ryan's life before he is taken to the Academy. DARK WEB is exclusively available to those in my readers' club – sign up for free at www.paulorton.net

RYAN JACOBS BOOK 1

Somehow, he lost his freedom.

Now he belongs to the Academy, and the rules have changed. What started out as a game has become a matter of life and death.

If he doesn't think fast, someone will die.

At thirteen you shouldn't have to face these kinds of issues. But at thirteen, you don't get to decide the rules.

THE RULES is the first book in the Ryan Jacobs series and is <u>AVAILABLE NOW ON AMAZON</u>!

Printed in Great Britain
by Amazon